Penelope Fitzger

is 'one of the finest and most entertaining novelists writing in England today' (Michael Ratcliffe, *Observer*).Three of her novels, *The Bookshop* (1978), *The Beginning of Spring* (1988) and *The Gate of Angels* (1990) have been shortlisted for the Booker prize. She was awarded the Prize in 1979 for *Offshore*. Her most recent novel, *The Blue Flower*, was chosen as 'Book of the Year' more often than any other in 1995.

Mrs Fitzgerald has worked in journalism, the Ministry of Food, the BBC and various schools, including a theatrical school. She lives in London.

PENELOPE FITZGERALD

The Golden Child

Flamingo
An Imprint of HarperCollins*Publishers*

Flamingo
An Imprint of HarperCollins*Publishers*
77–85 Fulham Palace Road,
Hammersmith, London W6 8JB

Published by Flamingo 1994

9 8 7 6 5 4 3 2

This edition published 1997
First published in Great Britain by
Colin Duckworth 1977

Author photograph by Tara Heinemann

ISBN 0 00 654625 0

Set in Baskerville

Printed and bound in Great Britain by
Caledonian International Book Manufacturing Ltd, Glasgow

For Desmond

For Desmond

1

The enormous building waited as though braced to defend itself, standing back resolutely from its great courtyard under a frozen January sky, colourless, cloudless, leafless and pigeonless. The courtyard was entirely filled with people. A restrained noise rose from them, like the grinding of the sea at slack water. They made slight surges forward, then back, but always gaining an inch.

Inside the building the Deputy Director, Security, reviewed the disposition of his forces. The duties that led to congratulation and overtime had always in the past been strictly allocated by seniority, as some of the older ones were still, for the hundredth time, pointing out, grumbling that they were not to the fore. 'This is a time when we may need force,' the DD(S) replied patiently. 'Experience, too, of course,' he added conciliatingly. The huge bronze clock in the atrium, at which he glanced, had the peculiarity of waiting and then jumping forwards a whole minute; and this peculiarity made it impossible not to say, Three minutes to go, two minutes to go. 'Three minutes to go,' said DD(S). 'We are all quite clear, I take it. Slight accidents, fainting, trampling under foot – the emergency First Aid posts are indicated in your orders for the day; complaints, show sympathy; disorder, contain; increased disorder, communicate directly with my office; wild disorder, the police, to be avoided if possible. Crash barriers to be kept in place at all entries at all times. No lingering.'

'Sir William doesn't approve of that,' said a resolutely doleful voice.

'I fail to account for your presence here, Jones. You have

7

already been drafted, and your place, as usual, is in Stores. The real danger point is the approach to the tomb,' he added in a louder voice; 'that's been agreed, both with you and higher up.' The bronze hand jumped the last minute, both inside and on the public face outside the building, and with the august movement of a natural disaster the wave of human beings lapped up the steps and entered the hall. The first public day of the Museum's winter exhibition of the Golden Child had begun.

It was the dreaded Primary Schools day. The courtyards had been partitioned by the darkly gleaming posters announcing the Exhibition. On each poster was a pale representation, in the style of Maurice Denis, of the Golden Child and the Ball of Golden Twine, with much fancy lettering, and a promise of reduced prices of admission for the very old and the very young. The moving files wound, like a barbarian horde, among these golden posters: five or six thousand children, mostly dressed in blue cotton trousers once thought suitable only for oppressed Chinese peasants, and little plastic jackets; half unconscious with cold, having long since eaten the sandwiches which were intended for several hours later, more or less under the control of numbed teachers, insistent, single-minded, determined to see and to have seen. Like pilgrims of a former day, they were earning their salvation by reaching the end of a journey.

At one point in the courtyard a faint steam or smoke, like that of a camp-fire, rose above the cloud of breath from the swarming red-and-blue-nosed children. It was the field kitchen of the WVS, with urns at the simmer, strategically placed to help those who might otherwise collapse before they reached the steps. Here they all paused a moment, drank an inch of hot catering tea, sweetened at too early a stage for any choice to be made, threw down their plastic cups on the frozen ground and then advanced over what soon became a carpet of plastic cups, blowing on their stiff hands in order to turn the pages of the catalogue which they already knew by heart.

They were not ignorant, these heroically enduring thousands. On the contrary, they were very well informed, and had been for months, as to the nature and content of the Treasure, past which they would file today, perhaps for thirty minutes.

> Life among the Garamantians was not really much as we know it today due to their living in Africa in 449 B.C. (HERODOTUS) says they did this. They exchanged gold for salt. (HERODOTUS) says they did this. They had gold, other people had salt, contrary to what we see in England today. They buried their Kings in caves in rocks. So the caves were (TOMBS). When the King was a small child they buried him in a small cave. The dead body was covered with gold. He had a ball of golden (TWINE) to find the way back from the Underground. This was confusing, as is the London Underground. Twine is what we call string, but the Garamantians used different words, due to living in Africa in 944 B.C. When they spoke the sound was likened to the shrill twittering of a bat. Well, personally I have not heard a bat, but it is a Faint Shriek. The child also had Golden Toys put with him to play with after death, as there was no way for him to have proper things – bikes, choppers etc. – as we know them today. I will end here as sir has told us to give in the (CATALOGUE).

The above, one of many projects faithfully carried by their authors to the source of knowledge, was accurate as far as it went. Of the Garamantes Herodotus tells us that they lived in the interior of Africa, near the oases in the heart of the Sahara, and that 'their language bears no resemblance to that of any other nation, for it is like the screeching of bats' (*nukterides*). Twice a year, when the caravans of salt arrived from the north, it was their custom to creep out without being seen and to leave gold in exchange for the salt, for which they had a craving; if it was not accepted, they would put out more gold in the night, but still without allowing themselves to be seen.

They dried the bodies of their dead kings in the sun and buried them in coffins of the precious salt, hardened in the air to a rock-like substance and painted to look like the persons inside; but the corpse itself was covered with gold leaf, which does not corrupt, and since the Garamantians believed that the dead would like to return often, although they might not always be able to do so, they buried with them a ball of fine golden string, to wind and unwind on their journey to the unseen.

The schoolchildren also knew that the Golden Treasure of the Garamantes had been rediscovered in 1913 by Sir William Simpkin, then a very young man and, it must seem, considerably luckier than the archaeologists of today.

Sir William Livingstone Simpkin was born the son of a (MAINTENANCE ENGINEER) which was then called a stoker at a warehouse. They lived down by the old East India Docks. He was named after an explorer. Some say there is a fate in names. He did not go much to school and helped at the warehouse unloading the crates, similarly to what we do for Saturday jobs. Well, this crate had tiles in it from (LACHISH) which is mentioned in the Bible. Well, all these tiles had been sent for a great (ARCHAEOLOGIST) Sir Flinders Petrie. So he took a kindly interest in him. You could train for a bit at London University, he said. Then you would understand the writing on them tiles. So this was how he got started on his work. Unfortunately, his wife is dead.

Sir William, in extreme but clear-headed old age, and after a lifetime of fieldwork, had come to roost in the Museum itself. The vast building was constructed so that no one could see in through any of the windows; otherwise the little lean old figure, with large white moustaches like those of Sir Edward Elgar, might have been glimpsed at a desk on the fourth floor, gently turning the pages of a book. He would have been recognised, even though it was many years since he last appeared on TV, for his appearance had passed into popular mythology. His almost transparent ancient fingers lay across the sepia photographs and the letters and newspaper cuttings crumbling at the edges to dust.

Sir William was playing at defeating Time by turning his pages at random. Here, in the section of June 1913, was Al Moussa, the Chief Minister, who had been persuaded into allowing him to examine the tombs, on condition they were sealed again for ever. Al Moussa was smiling nervously, in formal morning dress, and with many medals; he had not lasted long. There, on the next page, armed with lethal old rifles, were the band of wild Kurds, expelled from Turkey, who had guarded the expedition across the desert, raggedly devoted to their master; all went well till the return to Tripoli, when the Kurds, deprived of their women for many months, rushed headlong into the brothel quarter, scattering their cargo of notes and scientific measurements to the wind.

'Poor fellows!' murmured Sir William.

He turned, for a few moments only, for he was quite without personal vanity, to the official photograph of the actual rediscovery of the tomb; he looked so young, like a scanty bundle of washing, it seemed to him now, there in his tropical whites, pointing to the blurred and shadowy entrance.

'Pardon me, Sir William, I wonder if you'd just take a look at this.'

It was Deputy Security who had trampled into the room and, awkwardly jotting the old man from past to present, laid a piece of bright yellow paper, a leaflet, on the open photograph album.

GOLD IS FILTH
FILTH IS BLOOD

Do you realise that there are People who are Manipulating you in their Own Interests and who are seeing to it that you go to the exhibition in your Millions in Spite of the fact that it is under a Curse. This So-called Treasure, which has been hidden from Mortal Eye for sixty years, is several times referred to in Holy Writ, where we are told that to 'look upon Gold is the Body of Death'. When the Treasure arrived on this soil, the Dockers and Transport Workers were not allowed to Move it by Order of their democratically elected Unions. Ask yourself, Why was This? The Truth is that those who look upon the Exhibition are doomed, and yet they are paying 50p for the Privilege. Know the Truth, and the Truth shall Save Ye 50p.

GOLD IS DEATH

'Where did this come from?' asked Sir William, always sympathetic, however inconvenient it might be, to genuine distress.

'They just seemed to appear from nowhere in their hundreds among the queues, all over the forecourt. One moment there was nothing, then these leaflets all over the place, wherever you looked. They're all picking them up and perusing them, sir.'

Sir William turned the yellow paper over in his thin old fingers.

'Is there any disturbance?'

'Well, a teacher fainted and hit himself on the steps, and there was a fair amount of blood, from the nose, the First Aid Room tells me, but blood all looks much the same if you haven't seen any before.'

'And what do you want me to do?'

'That's it, I've come to make a request – I accept you don't want to come down personally – '

'Did anyone suggest that I should? Not Sir John, surely?'

'Oh, no, sir, not the Director. It was Public Relations. But if you don't want to disturb yourself – if you could just issue some sort of definite statement – I mean, as the only real authority – something we could relay over the TA system –

something about the Treasure and the whole matter of this curse . . .'

Sir William appeared to be meditating.

'I expect that I could do that for you,' he said, 'but I am not sure of how much use it would be. First of all, you may tell them, with my authority, that every child who can collect fifty of these documents, and put them in the rubbish bins provided, will receive a pound note.'

'I shall have to clear that with Departmental Expenses,' said the troubled Deputy Security.

'I shall pay the money personally,' replied Sir William calmly, 'but, in respect of what has been called the Curse, I should like you to add this. Everything that grows naturally out of the earth has its own virtue and its own healing power. Everything, on the other hand, that is long hidden in the earth and is dragged by human beings into the light of day, brings with it its own danger, perhaps danger of death.'

The Deputy Keeper stood rigid with attention and dismay.

'That doesn't sound very reassuring, Sir William.'

'I am not reassured,' replied the old man.

Sir William had a kind of equivalent to the long-vanished band of wild Kurds in a solid, grizzled, flat-footed museum official called Jones, nominally one of the warding staff, either on stores or cloakroom duties, but in fact acting as a kind of personal retainer to the old man. It was felt that on Sir William's account, 'not much could be done about Jones'. This was a source of annoyance to the Establishment, Superintendence and Accounts Departments, but they had been asked for forbearance – it could not be for more than a few years now – by the Director, Sir John Allison, himself.

For this concession Sir William was grateful to Sir John. It made a kind of bond between the awe-inspiring, gently smiling, wondrous blend of civil servant and scholar, who had risen quietly and inevitably, though early in his career (he was forty-five) to the very top of the museum structure, and the ancient ruffian who lingered in a corner of the fourth floor. Without his countenance, of course, Sir William, whose job was undefined, could scarcely have been there at all, but it must be admitted (since everybody knew it) that there was another reason for Sir John's care and protection, which had its origins in the vital question of money. Sir William made no secret of his intention to leave a large part of his fortune – accumulated heaven knows how and invested heaven knows where – to the Director, to be spent as he thought fit in the improvement of the Museum. This, in its turn, would mean a vast increase in the Museum's holdings of French porcelain, silverware, and furniture, the centre of Sir John's working life – he knew more about this subject than anyone else in the world – and the centre of his emotional life also, for the two came to much the same thing.

Sir John was paying a brief call on Sir William, ascending in his private lift to the fourth floor, since the old man had to be spared walking as much as possible. Sir William had particularly asked to see him, being deeply disturbed at the plight of the frozen children and teachers, now gradually thawing and steaming as they reached the haven of the entrance halls.

'I went through a few rough times finding these things,' he muttered, 'but God knows if they were worse than what these people suffer when they pay to see them.'

Sir John wondered privately how the old man could know this, since he had positively refused to go and look at the Treasure on its arrival or to visit the exhibition.

Sir William read his thoughts without difficulty. 'When you've been in business as long as I have, John, you won't have to go out to get information, it will come to you.' The Director produced out of his pocket something exquisite – a box containing a tiny but priceless feast-day Icon from Crete, a saint in jewelled robes raising a man from the dead. 'The box was made for it, of course. One thinks of the Prado, but theirs was stolen, I think.'

The two men bent over it, absolutely united, and for a

moment suspended in time and place, by their admiration for something fine.

'Have you had any coffee?' the Director asked, shutting the little box.

'Well, Jones brought it, I suppose.'

'Where's your secretary, where's Miss Vartarian?'

'Oh, Dousha has to come in late these mornings, she has to be indulged. You only have to look at her to see that.'

'She ought to be in. You haven't forgotten it's a Press Day? We shall be bringing this Frenchman, this anthropologist, along to see you later. And there's the Garamantologist, German I suppose, but the combined efforts of my staff haven't really discovered what his nationality is – Professor Untermensch, I mean.'

Sir William gazed at the Director like an old tortoise. 'I know all that, John, and what's more, in case I should forget it I am to receive a visit from your subordinate from the Department of Funerary Art, Hawthorne-Mannering.'

'He means well,' said the Director.

'Nonsense', replied Sir William, 'but let him come, let them all come. I dare say I shall be able to forget enough to keep them happy.'

It was one of Sir William's difficult days, and yet surely he was no more difficult than anyone else. The Museum, nominally a place of dignity and order, a great sanctuary in the midst of roaring traffic for the choicest products of the human spirit, was, to those who worked in it, a free-for-all struggle of the crudest kind. Even in total silence one could sense the ferocious efforts of the highly cultured staff trying to ascend the narrow ladder of promotion. There was so little scope and those at the top seemed, like the exhibits themselves, to be preserved so long. The Director himself had been born to succeed, but he now had to have a consultation, at their request, certainly not at his, with two of the Keepers of Department who had been expectant of promotion long before his arrival, and who regarded him with a jealousy crueller than the grave.

Sir John was immune from the necessity of being liked. He went down one floor in his private lift. A nod from his invaluable private secretary, Miss Rank, indicated that the loathsome pair must have already arrived, and, as befitted their seniority, had been shown into his private room.

The Director took his place behind his rosewood desk, the beauty of whose inlay might have made it fit for the Wallace Collection. As a matter of fact it *did* belong to the Wallace, and one of Sir John's few weaknesses was revealed in his very long delay in returning it after a loan exhibition. The two Keepers opposite him, quite impervious to the delicate, fruit-like shimmer of the polished wood, were Woven Textiles and Unglazed Ceramics. They sat close together, like conspirators.

'I'm a moment or two late, you must both forgive me . . .'

'It is, as you well know, simply the matter of Sir William's bequest. The suggestion seems to be that he is not likely to last very much longer?'

The Director gazed at their skull-like faces. How long did they expect to last themselves? But he acknowledged that they were indestructible. They had been there when he came. They would also be there when he left.

Unglazed Ceramics tapped menacingly on the gleaming desk.

'We take it that the bequest, which it now seems will be very considerable, will be evenly distributed among the departments? This would normally be a matter for the Trustees, but since it is to be administered by you personally . . .'

'A rumour is circulating – one might put it higher than that – that expenditure will be concentrated on only one of the Museum's collections . . .'

'. . . a rumour which is circulating among art dealers and art investment companies . . .

'. . . we, of course, entirely discount it . . .

'. . . but we feel that you are perhaps too busy to realise

the general surprise and disappointment at your failure to form a committee . . .

'. . . a small steering committee, on which we are both ready to serve . . .

'. . . to see that the needs of all departments, as far as possible, are fairly considered . . .'

Sir John looked at them with unwavering courtesy. He saw them as two old fakirs, one sitting on a pile of rags, the other on a heap of cracked pots and broken earthenware. Even more deeply than ever did he resolve that every penny the Museum could legitimately acquire should go to the superb artefacts of the *dix-septième*.

The Keeper of Woven Textiles indicated a heavy pile of typescript.

'I have prepared a kind of aide-memoire, simply indicating acquisitions that might be made in the near future, or even reserved now . . . there is, in particular, a silk kashan, knotted in 1856 . . . an important example . . . a favourable moment . . . information from Beirut . . . many Lebanese collectors are de-accessionising . . .'

'Excellent,' said the Director. He particularly hated Oriental rugs, which took up an immoderate amount of display space. 'It's good of you to give me a summary of priorities, though naturally I am fairly well aware . . .'

'You misunderstand me, John. That is *my* list; my colleague here has brought his own, of course.'

Of course. Another weight of closely typewritten pages.

'Can we take it that we have made our point?'

'Indeed you can. But in any case you can rest assured that I am thinking about the formation of a consultative committee to discuss the preparation of a report to recommend the appointment of a special purchasing committee. The name of Lord Goodman suggests itself. I shall be seeing him this week . . .'

With practised phrases the Director steered the two gibbering Keepers back towards the dark tomb-like sanctuary from which they had so inconveniently emerged. Miss

Rank rose from her place, knowing without request what was needed, to escort them on their way.

Left to himself, Sir John mused that the Exhibition, which had been intended to fulfil so many hopes, was already on its way to distilling bitter hatred, not only on a departmental, but on an international scale. The decision to mount it in London was surely a justifiable one – since the caves had been resealed, Sir William's book was, and presumably would remain, the only scientific account of the cave burials. But the International Council of Museums had not been consulted. Both Paris and New York had expected priority, and there had been violent recrimination, or, as *The Times* put it, 'Discord in the Realms of Gold.' Once again it had been in mysterious circumstances that the Government of the present Republic of Garamantia had agreed to, or perhaps proposed, the loan of their priceless possessions. Sir William's name, although he had had absolutely nothing to do with the Exhibition, was again invoked, and it had been uncertain who was paying the bill and even exactly what was happening. A party of harmless experts and a roving BBC newsman were deported from Africa. Then, after further wearing disputes over protocol, handling, packing, supervision and insurance, and a general warning from the Ethics of Acquisition Permanent Committee, the huge cloth-wrapped crates arrived, without any proper notice being given, at Gatwick. In the confusion and secrecy of the landing there had been little chance for the interested world of scholarship to take part. Historians, archaeologists and Garamantologists retreated, grumbling, as the two Keepers had done, into the depths of their professional organisations.

Meanwhile, Marcus Hawthorne-Mannering was preparing himself to have, in his turn, a few words with Sir William.

Hawthorne-Mannering, the Keeper of Funerary Art, was an exceedingly thin, well-dressed, disquieting person, pale, with movements full of graceful suffering, like the mermaid who was doomed to walk upon knives. Born related, or nearly related, to all the great families of England (who wondered why, if he was so keen on art, he didn't take up a sensible job at Sotheby's), and seconded to the Museum from the Courtauld, he was deeply pained by almost everything he saw about him. It was said that he was born into the wrong century, but what century could have satisfied the delicate standards of Hawthorne-Mannering? He was very young (though not quite as young as he looked) to get a Department, but then it was not the Department he wanted; his heart was really in water-colours, not in the coarse objects, often mere ethnographica, of which he must now take charge. His appointment had been, in a sense, an administrative error, or perhaps a last resort; still more so had been the obscure manoeuvres by which the direct responsibility for the Exhibition for the Golden Child, in spite of its numerous consultative, financial and policy committees, had ultimately been landed, nominally at least, on the small Department of Funerary Art. Among the many sufferings of the now terribly overworked Hawthorne-Mannering was the necessity of seeing a good deal of Sir William. He disliked the old man and, again in a sense (this was a favourite phrase of his, shrinking away with a snails'-horn delicacy from complete commitment) he disapproved of him; he didn't like Sir William's ill-defined relationship to the museum structure; he envisaged him, like some antique monster, stretched across the entrance to his opportunities. 'The position is quite anomalous,' thought Hawthorne-Mannering, who, though tired-looking himself, dreamed of revitalisation, trendy special exhibitions and so forth. 'Why is one not surrounded with choicer spirits?'

It was Deputy Security who had asked him to see Sir William. It appeared that there was a certain report on the subject of the Exhibition, circulated at Cabinet level, of which Sir William, out of courtesy, had been sent a copy. It was probable that he had never read it, but since he was known for his tactless generosity in sharing information, and today was Press day, a few words of caution would be advisable. Hawthorne-Mannering had observed acidly that this document, whatever it was, had certainly not been disclosed to mere Keepers of Departments, and asked Deputy Security why he could not speak to Sir William himself. Deputy Security replied that he might look in later, but that with an estimated four thousand five hundred visitors on his hands he was very busy. The grotesque egoism of this left Hawthorne-Mannering speechless.

To reach Sir William's den-like office he had to encounter the sour looks of Jones, just leaving with a tray of medicines and a brandy-bottle. Then, in the secretary's room, he found that Dousha Vartarian had arrived. Dousha, curled in creamy splendour in her typing-chair, had the air of belonging completely, like a cat, to the space she occupied; this was in spite of the fact that her family were exiles from Azerbaijan. She was not at all like the Director's secretary, Miss Rank. She nodded sleepily to indicate to Hawthorne-Mannering that he could pass on and go straight in, but when he did so, he found Sir William's room empty.

The washroom door was open. He was evidently not there – only the usual thick haze of pipe smoke, for the old man smoked like a chimney. Hawthorne-Mannering had so very much not wanted to come that he felt unreasonably resentful. He glided to the window, and looked down two hundred feet to the slow mass of schoolchildren shuffling through the intense cold of the courtyard. At least one is warm, he reflected. An occasional icy wind stirred the posters so that they glinted like flecks of golden leaf. Through the glass the stream of information from the sound system could not be heard.

'What are you standing there for?' asked Sir William, suddenly appearing from a door marked OPEN IN EMER-GENCIES ONLY. 'Perhaps you thought you had something to say to me?'

'I did, although I haven't met with a very ready reception from – well, from your staff. That man Jones, for instance, appeared to look at me almost in a hostile manner . . .'

'Jones, oh, yes, he will do that. You'll have to get used to that, if you do much standing about here.'

'He perhaps thinks he is protecting you, but I should point out that it is by no means safe for you to go out on to the emergency exit platform.'

'It's the only place where I can get a view of the new aluminium box which they've put up in place, as far as I can see, of the old Papyrus Room, as a kind of canteen or pot-house for which the unfortunate public are now queueing four abreast.'

'It's a temporary measure, as I think you know, Sir William, to accommodate the enormous numbers. They are not, after all, obliged to come to the Exhibition.'

'They're obliged to feel that it's educational death if they don't. These booklets, with Golden Toys on the cover, these schools talks on the BBC, planned units for the Open University, Golden coach tours – the whole country has been persecuted to come here. And now they've got to queue for seven hours to get in. What would you say a museum is for?'

The minutes were slipping by, and there was so much to arrange. Hawthorne-Mannering succeeded in controlling himself. But of patience, unlike hate, one only has a certain store.

'The object of the museum is to acquire and preserve representative specimens, in the interests of the public,' he said.

'You say that,' returned Sir William, with another winning smile, 'and I say balls. The object of the Museum is to acquire power, not only at the expense of other museums, but absolutely. The art and treasures of the earth are gathered together so that the curators may crouch over them like the dynasts of old, showing now this, now that, as the fancy strikes them. Who knows what wealth exists in our own reserves, hidden far more securely than in the tombs of the Garamantes? There are acres of corridors in this Museum that no foot has ever trod, pigeons nesting in the cornices, wild cats, the descendants of the pets of Victorian curators, breeding unchecked in the basements, exhibits that are only looked at once a year, acquisitions of great value stacked away and forgotten. The wills of kings and merchant princes, who bequeathed their collections on condition they should always be on show to the public, are disregarded in death, and those sufferers trudging like peasants to the temporary canteen, to be filled with coconut cakes and to lift plastic containers to their lips – they pay for all, queue for all, are the excuse for all; I say, poor creatures!'

'Perhaps I might explain what I have been asked to see you about,' said Hawthorne-Mannering coldly.

'Well, I know that it's journalists' day, and you want the old lunatic to talk to them,' said Sir William, with a rather alarming change of tone. 'Bring them in, by all means.' Then, reverting to the language of his boyhood, he added, 'I'm careful what I say to them bleeders.'

Hawthorne-Mannering adroitly took advantage of this opening to point out the necessity for strict security. But Sir William continued musingly.

'Carnarvon died at five minutes to two on the morning of the 5th of April 1923. I knew him well, poor fellow! The public enjoys the idea of a curse, though. Why shouldn't they get what they can for their money?'

'But this is in no sense relevant, Sir William. I have no competency whatever to discuss the excavations of the Valley of the Kings, but I am sure that no responsible authority has ever attached any importance to the Curse of Tutankhamen, still less to the quite arbitrary invention by popular journalists in these past few weeks of the Curse of the Golden Child.'

'Who put those yellow pamphlets about?' asked Sir William. 'Gold is Filth? 50p?'

'I am afraid that is quite outside my – '

'Have you ever been under a curse?' asked Sir William.

'I think not. Or if so, I was not aware of it.'

'It's a curious feeling. It has to be taken seriously. By the way, I've forgotten your name for the moment.'

'The two journalists whom I am particularly recommending to you,' said Hawthorne-Mannering, ignoring this, 'will, of course, not wish to discuss the alleged curse or anything of a popular nature. They are the accredited archaeological correspondents of *The Times* and the *Guardian*. One of them, Peter Gratsos, is a personal friend of mine from the University of Alexandria. Louis Sintram of *The Times* you of course know.'

Sir William showed no signs of doing so.

'A chat, yes, about these trinkets, eh? There were deaths, you know, in 1913, though we never talked about them. Poor Pelissier was dead when we found him, with one of the golden toys in his hand. He was stiff as lead.'

'You will recall that the interview is to take the form of a short talk by Tite-Live Rochegrosse-Bergson from the Sorbonne – the distinguished anthropologist, anti-structuralist, mythologist and paroemiographer. Then there is Professor Untermensch, at present I think at Heidelberg. He has been invited, at his own request, to sit in. You are to make a few comments, a summing up, call it what you will . . .'

Sir William discharged a volley of foul smoke from his pipe.

'If you want me to say what I think about Rochegrosse-Bergson . . .'

'Hardly *about*, Sir William, but *to*. The whole discussion is to be on the highest level . . .'

Hawthorne-Mannering looked as though he were about to cry.

There was a faint disturbance in the outer office as Dousha moved in her chair. She could be seen through the green glass like an ample under-water goddess, slightly dislodged. The Deputy Director of Security came in.

'Excuse me, sir. Just a word about the arrangements for this morning.'

So he didn't trust me, thought Hawthorne-Mannering bitterly.

'Ah, security,' said Sir William. 'Quite right. There's a Frenchman coming. Good fellows enough, but you don't want Frenchmen and gold too near each other. Remember all that trouble with Snowden.'

'This document, sir – your copy of the secret report which, according to our information, concerns the genesis of the Exhibition.'

'Did I have a copy?' Sir William asked.

'Our records show that you did, sir, a complimentary copy. You and the Director were the only two recipients in the Museum.'

'Well, Allison may still have his copy, if you want one.'

'With respect, sir, that is not quite the point. The report being, as I have indicated, at Cabinet level, I should like to be sure that it is in safe hands during today's interviews.'

Sir William had been known, more than once, to leave confidential papers in a taxi or scattered about the reading room of his club.

'Dousha may have mislaid it. Poor girl,' said Sir William. 'I've no idea why a girl like that was appointed as my secretary,' he added unblushingly.

'There are a number of minutes downstairs, sir, from yourself to Establishment, urging her appointment on grounds of hardship.'

'Paper! paper!' rejoined Sir William. 'Fallen leaves! Faded leaves! But I'll see to it. Yes, yes, I'll get it under lock and key.'

'The other matter is a little awkward, sir – rather personal. We are informed that this Untermensch is a bit of an eccentric.'

Hawthorne-Mannering stirred slightly, feeling impelled to come to the defence of all savants, and perhaps of all eccentrics.

'One might feel that last remark as somewhat reductive,' he said. 'Professor Untermensch is a noted

Garamantologist who has devoted much of his life to a study of the treasure without, of course, having actually ever seen it except in photographs and from parallel sources. One might call him a kind of saint of photogrammetry. He is, also, the acknowledged expert on the Garamantian system of hieroglyphic writing.'

Deputy Security's business in life was to secure the safety of the objects he guarded. Their value, and the sanity of the staff, of both of which he had a low opinion, did not concern him.

'To continue, sir. Our information is that Untermensch is, not to put too fine a point on it, pretty cracked. That's to say he is obsessed with the idea of holding one of these objects from the treasure, one of these golden toys or whatever, of actually looking at it close to and holding it in his hand. I don't know whether you yourself, sir . . .'

'Nothing to do with me,' said Sir William. 'I've made it clear enough, to you and to everybody else, that I've no intention of going down to look at it and no wish to see those things again on this side of the kingdom of shades.'

'The Director himself will arrange for Professor Untermensch to have a closer view of one of the objects,' interposed Hawthorne-Mannering. 'He is hardly, perhaps, of sufficient standing . . . but this courtesy is to be shown to him, since he has been so very persistent . . .'

'Well, in any case it's too many people to see on one day,' said Sir William, 'but have it your own way.'

Hawthorne-Mannering lingered uneasily on the way out to speak to Dousha.

'I'm afraid the old man has not been very well,' he said. 'At one point he failed even to remember my name. Has his heart been giving trouble?' He could not make his voice sound sympathetic.

'Not so much, I think,' Dousha calmly replied.

As he left Sir William pressed the intercom with an untrembling finger.

'I didn't like that fellow, Dousha,' he said, 'Why doesn't Waring Smith come and see me? What's become of Smith?'

Waring Smith, as a junior Exhibition officer, was not, or should not have been, of any kind of importance in the Museum. Sir William had taken notice of him at the tail end of a committee meeting, because he was young, normal, unimpressed, sincere and worried.

By a turn of fate, however, Waring Smith had recently been given a little prominence. While Hawthorne-Mannering had been on one of the numerous sick leaves which his delicate constitution demanded, Waring had been obliged, since it was a job nobody else wanted, to prepare the catalogue for a small display of funerary inscriptions from Boghazkevi, singularly dull to all but confirmed Hittitologists. By going down and standing over the printers, he had even seen that this catalogue was ready in time. The little success had recommended him for further work on the present great exhibition. It had, however, earned him the undying hatred of the returning Hawthorne-Mannering.

Yet Waring Smith was scarcely worth such concentrated resentment. He was not an exceptional young man. The average Englishman has blue eyes and brown hair, and so had he. From his grammar school he had gone on to spend three rather happy years studying Technical Arts at University. Locked in the canteen during a sit-in, he had met a young woman who was doing colour chemistry, and persuaded her without difficulty to share his narrow bedroom in the First Year block. They agreed without much resistance on either side to get married as soon as he got his first salaried job. He had asked himself, did he love Haggie? and an unsuspected second self had answered, Yes, he did.

Before his marriage Waring had found his life was one of progressive simplifications. After he had begun to live with Haggie he had seen much less of his other friends. To save housework they had taken off the legs of the bed and put it on the floor, and so on. His assessments mattered to him; he had specialised in Exhibition techniques and had worked hard. They went out once a week to see films by leading French and Italian directors about the difficulties of making a film. Then they bought cans of beer and some crisps, went back to their room and expanded warmly in the dark. Now that he was married, on the other hand, he found it rather difficult to think of anything else beyond his job and his mortgage payments. In order to continue living in a very small terraced house in Clapham South, with a worrying leak somewhere in the roof and a stained glass panel in the front door, he had to repay to the Whitstable and Protective Building Society the sum of £118 a month. This figure loomed so large in Waring's daily thoughts, was so punctually waiting for him during any idle moment, that it sometimes seemed to him that his identity was changing and that there was no connection with the human being of five years ago who had scorned concentration on material things. Furthermore, he was often in trouble with Haggie, who had to work in a typing pool, where her knowledge of colour chemistry was wasted, and felt that he should be able to get home earlier from the Museum than he often did. Yet Waring Smith had an instinct for happiness against which even the Whitstable and Protective Society could not prevail, and it was this instinct which Sir William had discerned and tried to encourage.

When Dousha rang down to Waring's ill-ventilated cubby-hole of an office to say that Sir William would be glad of a cup of coffee with him, Waring had to ask whether he could come rather later, as he had been told to go down and see how things were going in the Exhibition itself. He had to check with security and public relations, make sure that the display material was in place, and report back to Hawthorne-Mannering, still supposedly in charge of co-ordination.

At the sight of his tiresomely energetic subordinate, Hawthorne-Mannering felt his thin blood rise, like faint green sap in a plant, with distaste. He closed his eyes, so as not to see Waring Smith.

The closed eyes worried Waring a little, but he blundered on.

'You ought to go down there, HM, you really ought.' He had never quite known what to call Hawthorne-Mannering, who was too young – or was he? – for 'sir'. Throughout the whole building he was known as the May Queen, but Waring tried to put this out of his mind. 'It's an amazing sight,' he went on eagerly, 'I've made a few notes, if you'd like to see them.'

'How very much more than thoughtful of you. There will be no need, then, for you to tell me about it.'

'But it's worrying, honestly it is. They're sticking it out so well – the queues, I mean – you can't help feeling sorry for them. And when they get in they're getting caught in the bottle-neck – the entrance to the chamber of the Golden Child. They're only letting them in four at a time. It's like the Black Hole of Calcutta.'

'The point of your comparison escapes me,' said Hawthorne-Mannering. 'The bottle-neck, as you call it, whatever objections were made by Security, is of course a simulation of the entrance to the original cave itself, so that the general public can recapture the atmosphere two thousand years ago, at dead of night, when the pitiful sarcophagus was secretly carried to its final resting-place.'

'But they might go mad at any moment. Security knows that, but I don't think the authorities do. And the cafeteria! There's a life-size replica of the Golden Child in hardboard to beckon you in and even at this time in the morning there's nothing left but luncheon-meat rolls.'

'What is luncheon meat?' asked Hawthorne-Mannering, shuddering slightly.

'Why should they suffer like this?' Waring pleaded. 'Some of them have been all night in the train.'

Hawthorne-Mannering, still without opening his eyes, stretched out his long pale hands, turned them slowly over, and spread them out in one of his chosen gestures.

'One's hands are clean,' he said.

Waring reminded himself that if he did not keep this job, it was not at all certain that he would get another one, and that the whole question of his salary was constantly under the scrutiny of the Whitstable and Protective Building Society. He returned to his cubby-hole, and went rapidly through his correspondence, which represented the scourings of a great Museum, passed on from the other departments. A series of letters begged the Museum to join the campaign against the misuse of resources; a dinner was to be held, at £15 a head, where the menu was to be written on the tablecloth to save paper. The NUT wanted all the glass cases in museums removed, so that the exhibits could become a meaningful action area, and the children could pick them up and relate them to their daily lives. 'Why not?' thought Waring. 'It would pretty soon clear a bit of space.' A confidential minute from Public Relations referred to Professor Untermensch. Properly it was their business to entertain him, but apart from his great knowledge, which could be taken on trust, was he of any real importance? Could not the Exhibition Department take him out for a meal (Category 4 Grade 2) and perhaps an entertainment? As he appeared to be German, what about an operetta? A what, thought Waring.

He wrote careful notes on the letters and went to see if he could find someone to type his replies. He was in luck, and one of the girls was free.

'Where do you have your hair cut, Mr Smith?' she asked casually as she took his notes.

'I go to Samson and Delilah, in Percy Street, when I can afford it.'

'Yes, well, we girls think you look quite nice. It's getting a bit ragged, though.'

Perhaps Haggie could trim it for me, Waring thought, before I, a junior executive, become an object of mockery.

He took a letter of his own out of his pocket. Looking at the outside did not make it any different. The Whitstable and Protective reminded him that one of their terms had been that he should within six months replace nearly all the slates on the roof and repoint, repair, make good etc., etc., which work had not so far been notified to them as having been done. Waring Smith's salary was AP3 £2,922–£3,702 pa + £120 fringe, with £261 London Weighting (under review). He knew these figures very well, and repeated them to himself perpetually. They had seemed quite princely, when he got the job.

Having entrusted all the other letters to the typist, he went to see Sir William.

In the outer office he found Dousha actually asleep, in a quiet, cream-coloured heap over her desk. By her side was a pile of her work, and on top of that a file which she had evidently just put there. It had a green sticker on it, which Waring knew meant top secret, and the subject was the Garamantian Exhibition.

Through the glass door he could hear Sir William in the mid-stream of a conversation. Without any thought of concealment, but with very great curiosity, he began to read the file.

It began with a sheet of thick paper embossed with the address of HM British Embassy in Garama, on which was written, in an exquisite script:

	1. The Foreign Secretary
	2. FO Head of African Department
Head of Chancery to	3. The Minister, Department of Education and Science
	4. Director, Institute of Strategic Studies

We have, of course, not forgotten our Herodotus . . .

Γρήμαντες οἳ πάντα ἄνθρωπον φεύγουσι καὶ πάντος ὁμιλίην, καὶ οὔτε ὅπλον ἐκτέαται ἀρήιον οὐδὲν οὔτε ἀμύνεσθαι ἐπιστέαται . . .

This was partially covered by an attached note:

What the hell does the sod think he's talking about?

The next minute was typewritten, and read:

Garamantia has no oil, no natural defences, no army, no education, and no bargaining power. She is, therefore, unworried by representatives of UNESCO, the CBI and commercial diplomats. On the other hand the population, insofar as it is amenable to census, is rising by 2.5% a year. Resources are meagre, and the infrastructure can scarcely be said to be deteriorating as there has never been any. Capital is scarcer than labour, but 'labour-intensive' hardly describes the Garamantian working methods. More than half of the perfectly healthy work force sleeps the entire day. The present Government (paramilitary group of the uncles of the reigning monarch, Prince Rasselas, down to enter Gordonstoun in 1980) fears takeover, wishes to put itself under the protection of the Union of Central African Muslim States (relations with USSR friendly) but has been told (as a result of consultation with the East German publicity firm Proklamatius) that the only useful contribution they can make to ingratiate themselves with the Union is to exhibit the Golden Treasure, for the first time in history, in the capitals of the West. Hopefully this is to promote the idea of age-old etc. settled cultural ideals and will to some extent combat the extraordinarily powerful presentation of the Israeli case. Hence Garamantian treasure to be sent hastewise.

The next minute, from the Commercial Attaché, read:

Backing for insurance mounting and transit of the exhibits has been obtained from the Hopeforth-Best International

Tobacco Corp. It is agreed that no advertising material shall be displayed or implied, but Hopeforth-Best have given us to understand, in strict confidence, that they feel the association of their product with the much-reverenced Treasure through their widely-used slogan 'Silence is Golden – Light up a Middle Tar Content' will prove consumerwise of substantial effect.

A final note from the Foreign Secretary's office:

We must watch these tobacco people, but it is certainly a great coup for our diplomacy that the Treasure, which of course is going to Paris and West Berlin, should come to London first. A compliment to Sir William Simpkin may possibly be intended, but His Excellency will be congratulated.

Waring shut the file and replaced it by Dousha's elbow. He stood there, deep in thought, till the door opened and Sir William, with unwonted spryness, looked out.

'Reading the confidential files, are you? Well, why not, why not? The more people know these secrets, the less nuisance they are. I'd read it out at the conference, only I don't want to upset the Director's feelings. No, that wouldn't do.'

A young journalist, who was on his way out, smiled uncertainly.

'I'd like to thank you for the interview, sir . . .'

'Mind you file it correctly,' croaked Sir William suddenly. 'The function of the Press is to tell the truth – aye, even at the risk of all that a man holds dear. Remember to tell them that a camel always makes a rattling noise in its throat when it's going to bite; remember to tell them that. There's many a man who would be living yet, if he'd heeded that advice.'

'Sir William, all that was absolute rubbish,' said Waring, as the reporter made his escape. 'Every one of your expeditions was professionally planned and recorded. You're talking like an old mountebank.'

'I like a joke occasionally,' Sir William said. 'In any case, it's true about the camels. But my jokes – well, I find not a lot of people understand them now. Your Director now, John – he seems to understand them. I was having a joke with him yesterday.'

'Did he laugh?' asked Waring doubtfully.

'Well, perhaps not very loud. But that's enough of that. How are things going below? Do you think they really find it was worth coming?'

Waring described what he had seen, this time to a much more sympathetic listener. Sir William's whole countenance seemed to change, leaving him very old-looking, pale and serious. He shook his head.

'Have you had a look at these, by the way?' he asked, pushing forward the bright yellow leaflet.

'Yes, I saw one or two of them down in the main courtyard. I thought perhaps a religious maniac.'

'I don't know why madness should always be put down to religion,' said Sir William, folding the leaflet up carefully as a useful pipe-lighter. 'Let us confine ourselves to the good we can do here and now. As it happens, I've asked you up here to do a favour for me. I want you to spare an hour or so this evening to take Dousha out to dinner. You can see for yourself how tired she is. She's had a tiring time lately.'

'I don't see how I can possibly do that . . . I'm expected home, I'm afraid . . . And I'm pretty sure Dousha wouldn't want to go out with a married man with a mortgage . . .'

'If you weren't married, I shouldn't trust you to take care of my poor Dousha. It's an expensive business, however – she eats copiously. I don't want you to face ruin . . .'

Sir William took a handful of coins out of the pocket of his coat, a long Norfolk jacket of antique cut, and sorting through some Maria Teresa dollars and Byzantine gold nomismata he produced a quantity of sterling. With difficulty Waring got him to put away the varied hoard, assuring him that it wasn't like that – Dousha and he would pay for themselves – and found that he had ended by accepting the absurd commission; he would have to go out with Dousha, whom he scarcely knew, and would be obliged to ring up Haggie and make what excuses he could.

With the handful of money Sir William had taken out of his pocket there was a small clay tablet, which was still lying on the desk. It was a palish red in colour, unbaked and unglazed, and covered with deeply incised characters. Waring felt almost sure that it was from the Exhibition.

'Ought that to be in your pocket, Sir William? Surely it's from Case VIII?'

'Quite possibly. I asked Jones to fetch it up for me last night.'

'But I thought you didn't want to see the Treasure again? You said you were too tired.'

'I am tired,' said Sir William, 'but that's not the reason, no. Regret is a luxury I can't permit myself. Let yourself go back into the past when you're an old man, and it will eat up your present, whatever present you've got. I was a great man then, or thought I was, when I saw the Treasure for the first time. That was sixty years ago. Let it stay sixty years ago. That's where it belongs.'

'It would be a wonderful thing for everyone down at the Exhibition, all the same, if you changed your mind.'

'I shan't change it. I just took a fancy to have a look at one of these to see to what extent I could still decipher the script. I knew it well enough at one time.'

'There's a copy of the Ventris decipherment downstairs in the staff library,' said Waring eagerly, 'and the Untermensch commentary, which gives you the whole alphabet.'

'I don't use libraries,' Sir William replied. 'When I was younger I thought, why read when you can pick up a spade and find out for yourself? I've published a dozen or so books myself, of course, but now I don't agree with anything I said in them. As to the Staff Library here, I might just as well throw away my key: they don't allow you to smoke in there.'

Waring tried in vain to envisage the old man without the wreaths of ascending haze from his briar which, even when he was half asleep, partially hid him from view. And yet, come what might, he felt it was a privilege to be smoked over by Sir William.

'I know you've got to be off, Waring, and earn your living. But just tell me this. Do you feel anything's wrong?'

Waring wondered exactly what this meant – the mortgage, about which he had confided in Sir William, or more likely the curious atmosphere of expecting the worst which had existed in the Museum ever since the first unpacking of the Treasure. He could only answer, 'Yes, but nothing that I can put right.'

He returned to his work. He had to submit suggestions for the layout of the counters in the new selling hall. The public desire to buy picture postcards had reached such a pitch (15,000 Get Well cards representing the Golden Tomb had already been sold) that it was necessary to clear new premises. A large court off the entrance hall had been pressed into service; it had been filched by the administration from the Keeper of Woven Textiles, who was left gnashing his few remaining teeth. Waring laid out his sketch plans, wishing he had rather more room, and wondering if he could ask to move for a while to the Conservation studios, where there was more space.

He had leisure now to think seriously about the report he had read, and over which Dousha had gone to sleep. He had a glimpse for the first time of the murky origins of the great golden attraction: hostilities in the Middle East, North African politics, the ill-coordinated activities of the Hopeforth-Best tobacco company. Perhaps similar forces and similar shoddy undertakings controlled every area of his life. Was it his duty to think about the report more deeply and, in that case, to do something about it?

Advancing cautiously into this unknown territory, he

thought first of his job. He frankly admitted to himself that he would have to be very hard pressed to do or say anything that would endanger his position as an AP3. Secondly came his loyalty to the Museum, a loyalty which he had undertaken, whatever his irritations and disillusions, to the service of beautiful objects and to the public who stood so much in need of them. Lastly he thought of Sir William, who, after all, had read the file and apparently attached no importance to it whatsoever. This was a comforting reflection. Let us pity women, as Sir William had said, and let us not worry too much about our manipulators, for whereas we have some idea of what we really want to do, they have none.

He spent part of his lunch hour telephoning home.

'Haggie! Is that you? It's your half-day, isn't it? No, well, not this evening, because something's come up.'

'Is it to do with Dousha?'

'Look, Haggie, I didn't know you'd ever heard of her. She's just Dousha, just Sir William's secretary. I'm sure I've never said anything about her.'

'Why haven't you?'

'This is stupid. I don't know her, and I don't want to go out with her. It's just that I don't feel I should disappoint Sir William. No, Sir William can't take her out, he's too old. I can't think what we're talking about. She's asleep half the time, anyway. I love you, I want to come home.'

Haggie had rung off.

In the great hive of the Museum, with the Golden Treasure at its heart, the mass of workers and young ones below continued to file, even during the sacred lunch-hour, with ceaseless steps past the admission counter. The long afternoon began. Above in the myriad cells drones, cut off from the sound of life, dozed over their in-trays. But Hawthorne-Mannering, neurotically eager, spent no moment in relaxation. Dr Tite-Live Rochegrosse-Bergson and Professor Untermensch had both arrived, though separately, had been conveyed from the airport in the same car – rather a shoddy manoeuvre, obscuring the inferior importance of the little German – and were now at the Museum. Elegantly groomed, like an attendant wraith, Hawthorne-Mannering urged them towards the passage and the lift for their conference.

'. . . in Sir William's room . . . a few words with two selected journalists . . . my good friend Peter Gratsos . . . Louis Sintram of *The Times* you will know of course . . .'

Rochegrosse-Bergson was a finished product, silver-haired but unmarked by time, wearing a velvet blazer and buckled shoes which could have belonged to one of several past centuries. The aura of one with many devotees, and – equally necessary to the Academician – many enemies, to whose intrigues in attempting to refute his theories he gracefully alluded, hung round about him. Professor Untermensch was smaller, darker, much quieter and much shabbier, but, on close examination, much more alarming, since he could be seen to be quivering with suppressed excitement. His jerky movements, the habitual sad gestures of the refugee, were accentuated, and his nose, as he humbly followed in the steps of the others, twitched, as though on the track of nourishment.

'Could I have a word with you, Mr Hawthorne-Mannering?' asked Deputy Security, suddenly advancing on the little group up an imposing side-staircase paved with marble.

'It's not at all convenient at the moment. Frankly, I find all these security precautions somewhat exaggerated. One's distinguished visitors from abroad are disconcerted . . . After all, it's not as though there were any specific trouble . . .'

'That's what I wanted to mention to you, Mr Hawthorne-Mannering. The police are in the building.'

2

'The police! One imagines they may well be here constantly, with the vast intrusion caused by the Exhibition . . .'

Hawthorne-Mannering realised at once that 'intrusion' was not the word he should have chosen, but he was too proud to change it.

'If you could step in here, sir, just for a word with the police. Mace is the name – they've sent Inspector Mace from the station.'

'But one's guests . . .'

'I could take them to the staff cafeteria if you think fit, for a glass of wine before the conference.'

This was a handsome offer from Deputy Security, but Hawthorne-Mannering received it with a finely-tuned suggestion of irritation.

'I have already given them a glass of wine, though not from the staff cafeteria. I don't know that Untermensch should have any more. He might easily become tipsy.'

Inexorably Deputy Security led the two savants away, while Hawthorne-Mannering was left in a small, almost disused room off the corridor, lined with cases containing some hundreds of Romano-British blue glass tear-bottles. Inspector Mace, more solid than anything else in the room, rose to meet him.

'Well, Inspector, I hope you won't regard it as offensive if I say that one is rather in a hurry . . .'

'Quite so, sir. I've no intention of wasting time, either ours or yours. It is simply that due to increasing our force patrolling the area during the Exhibition it has been reported in passing by one of my men that cannabis indica is being illegally grown on one of the ground floor window sills of the Museum. This, as you know, is a serious offence.'

'In what possible way, Inspector, can I be concerned with this?'

'We have been given to understand, sir, that you're in charge of the Department of Funerary Art. The cannabis was being grown in what I am given to understand are known as "death pots", that is, large funerary urns from your department. They were put just inside the window in an empty room to get the benefit of the central heating.'

'With the Museum full of gold, you bother about two pots! If you mean to say that this is my sole connection with the affair . . .'

'Have you noted down two pots as having gone missing, sir?'

'The Museum has a holding of several thousand urns. Very few are on show at one time. I have not checked them personally for some months . . .'

'I see. Meanwhile, perhaps you could inform us as to whether there are any registered addicts among your personnel?'

'I can only say that I regret I am unable to help you. I recommend you to apply to Establishment, who engage the clerical staff. Meanwhile I recommend you, or implore you, or what you like, not to take any further steps until the Exhibition has been running a few more weeks. One has enough on one's hands already.'

'I am afraid we shall have to press the charges, sir,' said Inspector Mace, but hesitation could be detected beneath his firm exterior. 'The preliminary steps might, perhaps, be deferred a week or two. Of course, sir, we don't wish to interrupt the wonderful public service the Museum is doing, in welcoming thousands of ordinary folk and giving them an opportunity to share its treasures . . .'

Escaping from the Inspector, Hawthorne-Mannering ascended with flying steps to Sir William's room. The conference had already begun. Dr Rochegrosse-Bergson and Professor Untermensch had understandably declined the opportunity of a visit to the staff cafeteria, and had proceeded direct to the conference. All were seated, and the telephone had just rung, so that Miss Rank could signify that the Director was almost ready to join them. In another minute she rang through again, to say that he was on his way.

The queue, when Sir John glanced at it from the arched window which shed a chilly light into the corridor, looked tranquil enough. Frozen into submission, another fifty schools were marshalled into line, 'closing up' at every opportunity to give an illusion of forward motion. Round the WVS coffee-stall the ground-frost had now melted, making a dark circular pattern. The whole area had become littered with plastic cups and spoons. Everything was orderly, there was no trouble at all.

The Director was well-known for his astounding power of cutting off his attention from one subject and focussing it on another, as a result of which, by the way, he had made a number of rather unwise decisions. But it enabled him now to forget both the enormous and the petty problems of administration as he entered Sir William's room and looked round the assembly. The two journalists, exquisites for whom life could hold no further surprises, and removed by their foreign education from crass British prejudices, sat in their Italian silk shirts and deerskin jackets, waiting, in a kind of energetic idleness. Sintram had folded his long legs and placed one well-turned ankle on the opposite knee. Hawthorne-Mannering, pale as alabaster, was evidently dreadfully fussed. Sir William, having risen to greet the French and German scholars, had slumped down low, alarmingly low, in his easy chair and almost disappeared in his cloud of pipe-smoke, depriving them of the formal speech of congratulations which both had intended to make. They were opening their brief-cases.

Rochegrosse-Bergson's white hands slid over the golden clasp; the Professor's case was shabby, and fastened with an unyielding zip. He sat altogether in the background, unconsidered and largely unaccounted for. As soon as the Director came in he fixed his sharp little eyes on him and concentrated on nothing else.

With the ease of long practice – evidently he could have lectured from a housetop, or in the middle of a desert – Rochegrosse-Bergson, in fluent English, commenced his discourse. After an *entrée en matière*, lasting a quarter of an hour exactly, he proceeded to a refutation of his unseen enemies.

'Let us admit that Man, when he looks round at the world, tries, as his nature demands, to put some order or pattern into the confusing mass of objects he sees. What is this order? It is the error, the childish error of structuralists to believe that we divide all our concepts into twos, and only into twos. Mentally, do we not on the contrary see everything about us in threes?'

'Some things look better in pairs,' Sir William said. 'They'd look odd if there were three of them.'

'Yes, the universe is trinary,' Rochegrosse-Bergson continued, courteously ignoring the interruption. 'Just as the Ancients conceived of Three Graces linked in a circle and the Manxman dreams of three legs, so life is an eternal triad – going out – coming back and going out again. To understand the myth I proclaim to you that we must fold it in *three*.'

He moved his dapper hands with the gestures of an expert laundryman.

'Compare the Ball of Golden Twine, for example, which, in my view, is the most important object in your distinguished exhibition, with the clue of thread given by Ariadne to Theseus – and again with the cat's cradle, a game, *chers auditeurs*, which, unlike string itself, has no end. What do we find? We find, gentlemen, that we go into the labyrinth to discover what we once were. Holding firmly the precious

41

thread of golden twine, we ascend to the upper air, but knowing that we shall have once again, one day, to return to the interior of our unacknowledged selves. The journey of humanity is a progression neither forward nor backward, but noward. All our thoughts are, to use my own word, my own chosen signifier, *la pensée-stop* – the irresistible impulse to *stop thinking at all.* Our art – for every man, let us admit it, is an artist – is *to achieve absolutely nothing!*'

Amazingly enough, this arrant nonsense was eagerly taken down by the two journalists. Their cynicism was gone; they appeared hypnotised. A serious résumé would evidently appear in the *Times Literary Supplement.* Trained in French lycées, they were unable to resist the rounded sentences which now dropped a couple of tones to announce the coming peroration.

'And thus, my friends, I have endeavoured to make perhaps a little clearer this evening . . .'

Broad winter daylight shone through the windows. The journalists scribbled on.

Professor Untermensch also knew, from long habit, the falling sound of the peroration. His time was coming; he was drawing nearer to the fabled gold to which, at one remove, he had devoted so much of his life's work. His eagerness was distinctly embarrassing. As the director rose he also got up, ready to follow him like a shadow.

Hawthorne-Mannering was in agitation, feeling that things were not being done properly. Nobody had been thanked.

'If you could just manage a few words,' he murmured, hovering over Sir William. 'If you could just make some acknowledgement . . . if you could recognise the name of Rochegrosse-Bergson . . .'

'Why should I?' asked Sir William. 'It may be somebody's name, but it's not his.'

Waring had received a message from the impeccable Miss Rank. She rang down. The Director required the Golden

Doll from the Exhibition, to show it, as he had undertaken to do, to Professor Untermensch.

'Isn't that really Hawthorne-Mannering's business? He's inclined to be a little touchy if he thinks I'm doing his job.'

'The exhibit should have been up here with us four and three-quarter minutes ago,' Miss Rank replied.

'But I can't go and open the cases until the public have left and the place is clear. I don't think you can actually have been down there. They're packed six abreast. It's impossible.'

'The object Sir John requires is not in the cases. I have checked that it has gone to Records. Your friend Len Coker is supposed to be making a scale drawing of it in the Records Studio, but he should have finished and sent it up long ago.'

'He's not exactly a friend of mine,' Waring protested feebly.

'Your quickest way is through the Library. The other route to the studios will mean over half a mile of corridors.'

'Yes, but – '

'You are not entitled to a Library key. I am aware of that. I have sent the keys down to you. Returnable, of course.'

At that very moment one of the messengers (Internal), flat-footed in his buff overalls, padded in and laid a glittering bunch of keys in the in-tray.

Waring took them dutifully. He was in trouble all round. There would be Haggie to console when he eventually got home, and he was within something and a quarter minutes of actually keeping the Director waiting.

The Library, as Miss Rank had observed, was for the use of staff of a higher grade than Waring Smith, who did not earn enough to consult the many thousands of costly reference books. Buried deep underground, it adjoined the resource centres, studios and laboratories. There was a lift, but its operations were uncertain; so Waring ran down the circular iron staircase.

43

'Hullo, Mr Smith. I didn't know they gave you access to down here.'

Jones was toiling up towards him with a large volume under his arm. 'I go to a lot of places that you can't,' he added. 'You'd be surprised.'

But Waring was not surprised. 'I suppose it's something for Sir William,' he said, knowing that Jones wanted to stop and show him the book, whose weight was visibly distressing him. The musty tome was, in fact, the first volume of Professor Untermensch's study of the Garamantian script, *Garamantischengeheimschriftendechiffrierkunst.*

'In German,' said Jones, 'something he took a fancy to. There's not a lot of people would want to read it at his age. He doesn't come down here, of course.'

'So he was saying only this morning.'

'I'd like to tell you something, Mr Smith. I can talk to you, because you're not a gentleman. Sir William won't last much longer. They won't let him.'

'He's eighty-five, you know,' said Waring, touched by Jones' confidence, but anxious to hurry on, 'and I'm afraid his heart isn't too strong.'

'We've a right to every hair on our head and every breath we breathe, Mr Smith. I don't know whether you've ever heard that said. It was the Thought for Today on the radio yesterday. But believe me, they won't let him.'

They parted, and Waring hurried on through the Library. There was not much temptation to linger there; the dignified, leather-clad reading-room of former days had been moved down here and had been partially transformed by the current safety regulations into a kind of spacious prison cell, with steel sliding shelving, ventilators protected by wire grilles and a row of regulators prepared to discharge water and chemicals in case of fire. There were two heavy metal doors at the end, one leading to the Director's private library, the other to the Conservation and Technical Services Departments.

In Conservation and Technical the staff, happily far

44

removed from the manoeuvres, triumphs and jealousies of the Museum itself, worked on apparently undisturbed. They photographed, glued and mended, decided what could not be cleaned, preserved small objects with a coat of polyvinyl acetate, measured the effect of age and damp, and took a careful record of all that the Museum possessed. Their services were highly skilled, and certain people were employed there, because of their expertise, who would not have been tolerated in the upstairs departments. Such a one was Len Coker, whose broad, short, almost square back and wildly curling dark hair Waring could glimpse now through his open studio door.

The door was always open, and Waring had time to reflect that although, as he had told Miss Rank, he was not really a friend, he did like him very much. Len Coker was an odd fish. He had trained as an engineering draughtsman, but had come here as a Museums Association student a year or so ago. Politically he was exceedingly fierce, holding views of the most extreme kind, and attending in the evenings, so he said, a course in Conflict Promotion; yet in personal life he was gentle and frequently embarrassed. As a copyist he was exact and delicate, but once his instruments were put away he was no longer neat-handed, but as blundering a breaker, loser and wrecker as was ever let loose on the helpless world of objects.

At the moment a faint scraping sound (Len liked old-fashioned mapping pens) suggested that all was safe; he was drawing. A number of carefully spaced objects lay on the high tables, from incised pebbles to a large eighteenth dynasty fish spear. The Golden Doll had pride of place. A strangely smiling little dolly with folded hands, it lay glittering in its fibre-glass case. Two jasper beads, something like tears on its cheeks, had given it the name of The Weeping Doll.

'Bugger off! You can't have it!'

Len did not look up from his work, and the remark was made in a kind of muffled roar.

'Just for an hour or two, Len. Let me have it, there's a good fellow.' Waring was conscious that he was speaking rather as though to a large dog. 'If you're half-way through, you can have it straight back when the Director's finished with it. I'll see to that myself.'

But Len had not even started the drawing. His objections were made on principle alone.

'It amounts to a conspiracy, that's obvious enough, to deny the rank and file of the Museum any real chance to observe and comment. That's admitted between us, I think. The whole treasure was unpacked and whisked into place. No one could study anything. This is the only scale drawing I've been asked to do, and now they're trying to hustle me. Experiments have been neglected. Priceless opportunities are being lost, or would have been if . . .' He paused blankly for a moment, and then went on. 'There's been no proper examination. There's been no analysis.'

'Surely you don't want them to perform an inquest on the Golden Child, like poor Tutankhamen,' said Waring. 'They'd need all manner of permission. We should never have got the Exhibition mounted at all.'

'There should be free access for all genuine enquirers. There were traces of wine and ointment and vegetable matter. Bound to have been. Those could have been analysed and tested. The cause of human knowledge could have been served. It's part of the atmosphere of unease and suppression that's eroding any kind of dialogue between management and staff. I'm even told the police have been called in on some trumped-up excuse.'

'I know why the police are here,' Waring said. 'Everyone's talking about it. It's because they've found cannabis growing in pots on one of the ground-floor window-sills.'

'Very likely they have,' Len replied calmly. 'As it happens, I grew it myself.'

'You did!' Waring replied, stunned. 'You!'

'May I ask what you think you mean by that standard bourgeois reaction? You, one of the few people I was

46

beginning to tolerate. You point the finger of accusation and blame at me?'

'It's nothing to do with blame. It was a bit of a shock, because I'd thought of you as a self-contained kind of person. You told me the other day that you wanted to free yourself from all physical desires – nothing too much, nothing you couldn't do without.'

'I shall make known to the authorities in my own good time any reason for growing cannabis indica on their premises,' said Len rather vaguely, 'and at the same time I shall put back the pots, which I borrowed, without his knowledge, from the Queen of the May and his Funerary pissing Art Department. The vital thing, I repeat, is to make oneself aware of the corruption from top to bottom of the Museum. Do you realise why this Exhibition was ever put on in the first place?'

'Yes,' said Waring.

'How did you find out?'

'I saw a report about it in Sir William's office, and I thought I might as well read it.'

Len seemed a trifle disconcerted, but recovered himself.

'There'll be nothing in it, by fair means or foul, that I don't know backwards. They're fools if they think they can keep secrets from an intelligent artisan, with the Union of Scientific Workers behind him. All I ask for is time, and day by day that is denied me. Now they talk about photographing all these things before the drawings are half done to my satisfaction. Worse still, they're going to send one of them across to the Museum of Man. Without my knowledge and consent. My fish spear!'

Lumbering down from his high stool, still locked in his dream, he snatched the unwieldly spear and made a wild pass in the air. He lost balance, the heavy ivory shaft seemed to take over control as he gyrated like a top and lurched forward, and one of the shining prongs fastened on Waring's left foot, wounding it and pinning it to the ground.

Len stared at it in deep interest.

'It's like Patrick! The so-called saint! A classic case for analysis. When he was preaching to the Irish! He leant on his staff and it went right through this fellow's foot! But this fellow said nothing, thought it was a religious ordeal, endured it without saying a word!'

'Well, I am saying a word,' shouted Waring. 'You clumsy bugger, get this out of my foot.'

Len immediately became sympathetic and even tender. He skilfully extracted the prong, put on a neat bandage, and handed Waring a pair of his hand-knitted socks, which were drying on the radiator. Waring seized the opportunity, while Len was still penitent, to appropriate the Golden Doll and carry it off to the upper floors.

Miss Rank received him coldly.

The Director could be seen at that very moment emerging from his private office, and Waring got a glimpse of Professor Untermensch almost clinging to him. How strange Untermensch looked, small and dark, gripping his briefcase, the sign of the undefeated intellectual, and looking in his eagerness like some bonze of an unknown religion, approaching the source of his devotion! Miss Rank looked with casual disapproval at Waring's hand-knitted socks, and at his limp.

'I've never seen you limping before, Mr Smith,' she said.

Waring reflected that Miss Rank and Len Coker, although far apart in every other point of view, were united in their disdain for the way the world was run.

The Museum had extended its opening time with an extra session, from six until eight; and throughout the building, now ablaze with lights, vast quantities of overtime were accumulated by officials, executives and warding staff, servants of the Golden Treasure. At eight o'clock the whole Museum seemed to gather itself together and sigh as melancholy whistles reverberated in its inmost recesses. The queue inward ceased, the outward current dispersed, half dead from fatigue, clutching unintelligible catalogues and trashy reproductions of the Ball of Golden Twine, while the loudspeakers reminded them of how great their privileges had been and urged them in return to be careful to drop no litter.

During the afternoon and evening Waring rang up home several times, but there was no answer; Haggie must be out. It was time to carry out his promise and to collect Dousha, whom he found wide awake and quite ready. Her typewriter was covered up for the night and the office was tidy, but Sir William, more alert and wakeful as the night advanced, was still at his desk. He gave Waring an amiable nod.

'Just look in here and have a word with me when you've seen that young woman home,' he said.

'Well, I shall have to be getting home myself . . .'

'Just look in and see me. It won't be as late as that. The difference between night and day is greatly exaggerated. What's wrong with your foot?'

This was something Waring did not want to discuss. A warm feeling for Len Coker persisted, and the accident with the fish-spear was difficult to explain in his convincing terms. Luckily Sir William, who could be so persistent, said no more.

Dousha, rarely seen either standing or walking, looked enormous, blooming and radiant. She was wearing a flowing garment, apparently patched together from many rags, and over it a number of shawls, and things that buttoned casually together. The effect was that of a princess in disguise.

Waring had drawn out ten pounds with his cash card from the staff bank and had decided, for the next two hours at least, not to worry. The truth was that he was looking forward to having something substantial to eat. He and Haggie had both seriously decided that they should spend as little as possible on food, which, after all, was unimportant – you felt just the same afterwards whatever you ate – and they never went to restaurants. But this evening, after all, was not his responsibility, it was simply to indulge a kindly impulse of Sir William's. He might as well make the best of it.

There was still plenty of coming and going in the entrance hall: nobody, however, that Waring really knew, except for Len Coker, wearing a Government surplus postman's raincoat, and presumably on the way to a meeting. For some reason he stopped as they passed him, stood his ground and stared fixedly. Perhaps he thought they were frivolous, or perhaps – Waring hoped – he was worried about the limp.

Since he would have to go back to the Museum afterwards, Waring suggested that they might go to a small place in the next square which he had heard Miss Rank say was quite good. As he walked with Dousha between the damp plane trees and misty street lamps he resolved that as soon as possible he would take Haggie to the same place.

The restaurant, having been formerly called the Bloomsbury Group, Lytton Strachey Slept Here, the Cook Inn, Munchers, and Bistro Solzhenitzyn, now bore the name of The Crisis. It was so small and hot that it was a matter for astonishment that anyone should want to enter it. The day's menu, although the same as every day's, was scrawled in an apparently improvised manner in chalk on a blackboard; the writing was so crowded that neither the names nor the enormous prices could be read in the dim light afforded by candles stuck with their own grease on to wooden boards. Ambisexual waiters in white trousers scrimmaged like gondoliers in midstream among the rocking tables and placed on the sacking tablecloths wicker basketfuls of coarse prison bread and tiny carafes containing a few mouthfuls of rosé, compounded of dregs from the glasses of the larger restaurant next door.

Waring and Dousha saw nothing to criticise and were prepared to enjoy themselves. Waring propelled Dousha forward by main force towards a table at the back of the room which was so inconvenient, being jammed under an Edwardian coat-stand, that it was still left empty.

Tacking after Dousha's ample figure through a trail of cutlery which her drapery swept from the gimcrack tables, he felt reduced to a nonentity. But how different it was when she subsided, with a smile so broad that it might almost have been a laugh. 'This is nice,' she said, looking contentedly through the reeking haze. It was not, but Dousha made it seem so.

Waring stared at the blackboard. 'Let me try and order something for you,' he said. 'I promised Sir William I'd look after you properly.'

The menu alternated strangely between French and Old English, *Boeuf en daube* being followed by the mysterious Dollops.

'It all looks a bit fattening,' he said, and then felt annoyed with himself, for he was automatically repeating a remark of Haggie's without thinking of the vast and already cushiony Dousha.

'Oh, it will not make any difference,' said Dousha calmly. 'Sir William is only worried that I do not have enough proteins. I am pregnant, you see.'

'Oh, Dousha, are you? I mean, are you all right, are you happy about it?' He hardly knew her well enough to ask her anything more specific than that.

'Of course I am all right. I am very well suited in my work. I do not do very much. Sir William met my father on an expedition to Mount Ararat. That was why he befriended me, for my father's sake, when I did not know what to do or where to go, and now I have a nice job and am pregnant. Maternity is the great happiness of a woman's life.'

'Was your father an archaeologist, then?' said Waring, not knowing what else to ask.

'No, he was wrestler, and my mother was tumbler.'

Dousha settled back in her creaking chair and ordered snails, tripe allegedly cooked in cream, and suet pudding with treacle.

*   *   *

Whatever faint and unacknowledged expectations Waring might have had from the evening were extinguished by Dousha's occasional allusions to her coming baby, but faced with her tranquil radiance, he could not help enjoying himself. He delivered her dutifully to the door of her flat above a Cypriot grocer's shop, and turned back to the Museum, the last duty in a very long day before he could make his explanations with Haggie.

There were still a number of lights burning here and there in the two front wings of the building. The courtyard had been cleared by mechanical sweepers and lay deserted under the freezing moonlight. The crush barriers were ready, at action stations, for the next day's multitudes. The main doors were shut fast. Waring showed his pass and was admitted through a side entrance into the Assyrian Galleries.

Here the lights were off, perhaps through an administrative error, and it was lucky that Waring knew the way so well. The gallery, with its gigantic human-headed bulls stretched out beside each other, was dark indeed. The moonlight penetrated through an upper clerestory, but only, like a pointing finger, to pick out here a wing, there an eye, and to gleam on the colossal heads which seemed to be rising slowly upwards, as ancient beings were said to do, from the regions below the earth. Waring had an absurd illusion that someone was in fact moving behind the statues. If so, they would be flitting soundlessly in the direction of the Exhibition. Waring thought he would like to call out and ask who it was, but he was afraid of making a fool of himself. The vast scale of the statues might, perhaps, have an effect on the nerves. Almost invisible, the winged and bearded creatures frowned down, neglected for the temporary gold of the Garamantes which had been carted through their domain.

Such fancies are inexcusable in an Exhibition officer. Waring wondered if the food at the Crisis had been altogether wholesome. If not, what about Dousha? The lift was not working and he toiled up the stairs, wondering how on earth Sir William would get down. Doubtless Jones, who seemed to be privy to all the secrets of the Museum, would get the lift working for him. There was no need to worry about Sir William, and yet he could not help it. However absurd Len Coker's tirades might be, it was true that in every department of the Museum, since the treasure arrived, there had been the same thrill of faint unease.

Sir William at this late hour was once again showing every one of the eighty-five years of his age. He was sunk in his desk chair like a blanched old fossil in a crevice.

'Thank you for coming, thank you for remembering to come back. You remind me, you know, of a young fellow who was very helpful to me, at Abalessa, or Tebu, I think . . .'

'I don't know how I can do that,' said Waring gently. 'I was brought up in Hayling Island.'

'Well, well, I'm old, I need reminding of things . . . Dousha's all right, is she? I only wanted her to have a treat for once. She's a good girl, she'll make an excellent mother . . .'

Waring hardly knew how to answer this, but the old man went on.

'I just wanted you to put this back for me. They're shut downstairs, of course, so it will only take you a moment.'

He held up the red clay tablet which Waring had seen earlier in the day.

'I shouldn't have had this. No desire to go and see all the things on show, but I fancied a glimpse – think I told you – of some of the writing, and Jones got hold of this for me. Just slip it back now for me and there'll be no fuss made, no question of it being missed . . .'

'Wouldn't tomorrow do? I haven't heard anything about a re-check, and the tablets aren't catalogued individually. They're all under Miscellaneous Finds.'

'At eighty-five I've had an unexpected pang of conscience,' murmured Sir William, 'and suppose this was the world's last night, or more probably my last night . . . only I'm not sure where Jones got it from . . .'

'Oh, the tablets are in the second room,' said Waring reassuringly. 'All together, with a flooring of desert sand, and blow-ups of the desert caves – atmosphere, you know. There aren't the same security precautions there as we've got in the inner room. They're not in a high security case at all – just in an old case borrowed from Romano-British. If it's really on your mind, I'll see to it now.'

He felt that the spirit of this old man who had befriended him was wandering somewhere between past, present and future. Clearly he was distressed. It wouldn't take twenty minutes to put the tablet back, and to try to get through to Haggie once again to explain the further delay. Nothing really.

For the second time that day Waring was given a bunch of keys – this time a complete set, quite unused, to the Exhibition – and Sir William once again produced the little tablet. It was about six inches by two, and surprisingly well preserved; its mysterious columns of picture-writing were sharp, as though the reddish clay had been incised only yesterday. There were dozens like it in the Exhibition. Waring put it carefully into an envelope, throwing away the unwelcome statement from the Bank which it had previously contained.

'Leave it to me. I'll look after it. No problem. Good night, now.'

'Good-bye, Waring,' said Sir William, who had begun to doze off.

Certainly there was no problem. Waring knew the layout of the Exhibition as well as anyone in the building, and felt quite confident that he could explain himself if the night patrol came round while he was opening the case. Jones, in any case, was likely to be on the premises in some capacity, until Sir William left, and could give his comforting explanation that Mr Smith did these things because he wasn't a gentleman. The job was as good as done, and he allowed Haggie and the question of the mortgage to occupy the conscious part of his mind.

He was already through Room 1 which was devoted to enormously magnified photographs from Sir William's book of the 1913 expedition mounted on display boards with boldly printed explanations, and arranged like a kind of open maze to lead towards the discovery of the Treasure. Now he was in the Exhibition itself, hushed as though in expectation of tomorrow's immense procession of curiosity, boredom and wonder. The main lighting was cut off automatically at night, but the illumination of some of the cases was working and threw up a faint blue glow, just good enough to see by.

Without difficulty or disturbance he opened Case VIII, put the tablet back on the artfully scattered heap, and locked the back. I hope Sir William won't want to borrow anything else, he thought. He had done enough for one day. He would be home in three-quarters of an hour.

A sudden impulse seized him to take another look at the coffin of the Golden Child. At the unpacking and assemblage, at the cataloguing and photography sessions and during day after crowded day, the Child had become nothing but a centre of coming and going. What did he really look like? Without any conscious decision, Waring turned and walked straight through the tablet room into the inner sanctum.

The Golden Child lay in its double coffin of crystallised salt, the top lid open, so that the inner one could be stared at. The likeness of a prince was shown in a ritual painting on the lid of the outer coffin, but the painting on the inner one showed the face of a child, wrinkled like a thing that had never been born and never allowed to die. Every wrinkle, however, was thickly covered with gold. This second lid, in turn, was just ajar, so that you could glimpse the tiny body wrapped in strips of linen cloth. In the case beside it were its collection of golden rattles and comforters, to console it on the long journey. There was an empty space labelled TEMPORARILY REMOVED, for the Weeping Doll which Waring had fetched earlier that morning.

Then he noticed something else. The Ball of Golden Twine, ready to lead the dead child back to earth again, was missing.

A horrible sensation attacked Waring in the nerves of the small of the back, as though the flesh was being sucked from his bones by fear. He heard a faint sound behind him. Well, look round and see what it is. Rather anything than that, he thought. In that instant the hard cutting edge of a string caught him round the neck and was pulled tighter till it hurt, and he felt his tongue reaching out of his mouth by itself for air and lost consciousness.

3

Before he could bring himself to open his eyes Waring heard amidst a confusion of noises which he knew were inside, not outside, his bursting head the unmistakeably gloomy voice of Jones.

'Coming round a bit, Mr Smith?'

'I'm going to be sick,' Waring said.

'You *have* been sick.'

Jones was mopping up. Waring's first connected thought was, this serves me right for eating all that expensive dinner without Haggie. Pieces of the thought broke off, shone and fell to the floor of his mind. His head was being sawn in two, the intense pain in his throat seemed to answer to the pain in his damaged foot. After a day's hard work as an AP3 (Museums), doing the best he could, he was a wounded object, a casualty, just about able to sit up.

'Someone strangled me,' he said.

'They began to, I'd say,' said Jones with kindly relish. 'They didn't get very far. They must have heard me coming from Stores. Just a little look round, I like to have at nights. You passed out, that's all. I don't say it's not painful.'

'Did you see anybody?'

'They could have gone out the other exit, the other end, if they had the keys.'

'I had Sir William's keys. Where are they? Did you pick them up?'

'There wasn't any keys here, to my knowledge. I was wondering how you got here, to tell you the truth.'

'They took them, then. I've lost the keys.'

'Don't worry about that. I can get another set for Sir William.'

That was all that mattered to Jones. It was too much for Waring to think about so many things at once. There seemed to be a band of fire round his neck. Jones helped him to his feet.

'I daresay you'll be sick again, Mr Smith. They say three times.'

'Who did it? What did they do it with?'

He leaned against the cool glass of the case. The Ball of Golden Twine, missing, he could remember that clearly, when he came in, was back in its place.

'They had time to do that.'

'Do what? Now, what are we going to do for you next? If you can sit here for a bit I can fetch you something from First Aid stores, or I can put the kettle on down there if you want something hot.'

The obvious course of calling in the doctor or the police simply did not occur to Jones, who always had as little as he could to do with either. Besides, he had his own explanation of the incident. The Curse of the Golden Child, to his mind, had begun to work.

'Say what you like, there's something in it,' he kept repeating.

Waring tried to thank him. He had an overwhelming desire to get home. His ideas were painfully trying to connect with each other. The old habit! Someone had gone for him twice in one day. Well, the first time Len hadn't particularly meant to hurt him. But how violent was he? How accountable was he for his actions? It wouldn't be like Len, though, to run for it. He was far more likely to stay and harangue both himself and Jones on the necessity of putting the world's deposit of art in the hands of the people. Still, he couldn't understand Len. What about the pot of cannabis? That was stupid. The only thing to trust was an underlying instinct that, in spite of everything, Len's intentions were good. Certainly he couldn't afford to lose his job. Who could, even without a mortgage? Wouldn't it be best, once again, to say as little as he could about his injuries? Fortunately Jones, of all the warding staff in the building, was the easiest one to ask for secrecy. A hint that the whole thing was an errand for Sir William, which was true after all, would be sufficient. And then, thank God, he could go home, throw himself on Haggie's tenderness and go to bed.

'I think I could manage to get home all right now,' he said.

'Take my advice and don't come in tomorrow. A bit of sick-leave never did anyone any harm. You look a bit of a wreck, though. Frighten them in the Underground, you will.'

Waring still had his overcoat on; he had never taken it off after leaving the Crisis. Jones helped him to button it up to the neck to hide the fiery marks.

'It's not so bad, Mr Smith. I don't say it doesn't hurt. You ought to wear an old sock round your neck if it's anything to do with the throat, a knitted sock, something like you've got on.'

With an effort, Waring looked down at them.

'They're Mr Coker's,' he said, remembering.

'Take a day off, and you'll find you're as good as new.'

'You certainly managed to come at the right time, Jones. I don't know what you can have thought, when you saw me lying there.'

'A bit of a shock, but don't worry about that. It all makes for variety.'

Waring was on the Museum steps. And what a night there was outside, with the moon moving now through a wild, torn and streaming sky! The calm was broken; there was wind now in the upper air. He breathed in deeply the smell of leaf-mould that penetrated the myriad pavements. He could go home. It would be about an hour's walk, through Westminster and over Lambeth Bridge, but he felt too sick to risk the Underground, even though by this time of night many of the passengers would be as battered and odd-looking as himself. No, he could walk. He was so tired that he could think of nothing else but sleep. His bed seemed to be walking alongside him, gesturing with its sheets and pillows.

The familiar corner, the Clapham All-Nite Delicatessen still open, the Bengali shop-keeper sitting patiently by his oil stove, the next turning, second right, twelve stairs up. He went into the flat without calling out. It was a maisonette, really, Haggie always explained. There were two letters on the kitchen dresser: one was from the Whitstable and Protective Building Society: he did not open it. The other had no envelope, it was a page from a shopping list pad:

> Dearest W. Caroline came. I talked to her and we both thought it incredible that you should be so incredibly thoughtless, only if it gets to that point there isn't much either of us can do about it. I know it is more fun for you to go out with Dousha sometimes, we agreed not to be tied, at least I think we did, at least Caroline thinks we did. Only you always seem to be staying late at the Museum now. I am going to stay with her at this flat she has now in Hackney. Will send the address later. I did the launderette as there was nothing else to do so you will have enough for next week. I want to sort myself out because just at the moment I am incredibly unhappy.

It was the language of Haggie's deepest emotions, and, unfortunately, not incredible at all. But Waring had reached the point where he could not feel even this. He lay down and slept too deeply for any nightmare to touch him.

'Something exceedingly disturbing has come to my notice,' said the Director.

Hawthorne-Mannering, unexpectedly summoned at nine o'clock the next morning, felt in his guts an acute twist of anticipation. It was not that he believed he had anything to reproach himself with. But his oversensitive nature was in perpetual expectation of a coming disaster, with himself as the principal exhibit, first stared at and pointed out, then shelved and forgotten. He smoothed back his hair with his cold dry hands.

'It's nothing to do with your work, Marcus,' Sir John continued. 'You are limited, certainly, but I have no criticism of what you are doing. I should not, however, have asked you to come and see me so early if this matter had not concerned the Exhibition, which, by a confusion which there is no need to recall at the moment, became the nominal responsibility of your Department.'

He paused to listen to the distant echoes of the bells, which indicated that in three quarters of an hour it would be time for public admission.

'What has happened is, in a way, simple, but quite appalling,' he continued, opening the right-hand top drawer of his desk. He laid on the expanse of blotting paper a small, immaculate golden object: the Weeping Doll. With one finger he gently stood it up, and the crystalline tears on its face sparkled as it seemed to rise to its splayed feet.

'You were, of course, at yesterday's conference?'

Hawthorne-Mannering nodded, staring at the dolly.

'You know Rochegrosse-Bergson well, I think?'

'Reasonably well. He was somewhat taken aback when . . .'

'Quite. That's not what I'm discussing now. And Untermensch?'

'Untermensch. I'm afraid I'd never met him before.'

'At the conference – did he strike you in any way as not quite normal? His manner? Did it occur to you that this was at all unusual?'

'I'm sorry to say I didn't take much notice of him. Of course, he's not in my field at all . . . One has had to study a good deal of Garamantology lately, but scarcely enough

61

to talk to a specialist ... one knew, of course, that he was going to see you privately shortly afterwards ...'

The Director paused. 'After yesterday's meeting I carried out the promise I had given earlier to Professor Untermensch, who of course has spent a lifetime in scholarly analysis of the hieroglyphic writing of Garamantia. I was informed that it was his long-standing ambition to hold and examine closely one of the artefacts from the Treasure. This, though possibly childish, was understandable. I asked the Exhibition section to send me up Catalogue No. 232, a child's toy, executed in gold and jasper, one of the grave-goods. You see it now on my desk. There was some delay in sending it up. When it eventually came, just in time, Miss Rank tells me, I handed it, with proper precautions, to Untermensch.'

'What did he say?'

'He didn't exactly *say* anything.' The Director flung out his arms abruptly. 'He *laughed*. Like this – Ah wah ha hee! Ah wah ha hee!'

The high-pitched peal of laughter split the air of the room with terrifying effect. Hawthorne-Mannering had not known that the Director was so good a mimic. The imitation was as close as a bird-call.

'I expected an apology. I told Untermensch that he was at liberty to speak in French or German, if he wanted to express himself more clearly. But he continued in English. He told me that in fact he did not know any language perfectly except ancient Garamantian.'

Hawthorne-Mannering had been unsettled by the laughter. 'And then?'

'He told me that this toy, this artefact, was not an original, but a replica. The Golden Bird, the Golden Drinking-Cup, the Golden Twine, are all replicas. The jewels are counterfeit. The sacred Mask and Milk-bowl are quite recent copies. The only genuine thing in the Exhibition – an exhibition with which the name of the Museum, and indeed the name of the British Government, is now deeply involved – are

62

those wretched clay tablets which litter the area and which, it seems, can be picked up for a few pence in the bazaars of Tripoli.'

'That's impossible!' cried Hawthorne-Mannering. But he seemed to huddle and shrink, as though transfixed by an arrow. 'Did you let him see everything?'

'As soon as the public admission closed. It didn't take him long to make an examination. I repeat, Marcus, why do you say it is impossible?'

'A thousand reasons. You must have been through them already. You know them so much better than I do. The Garamantian government, the insurance people, the experts over there who supervised despatch, the Diplomatic people, the experts over here, everyone, every mortal reason.'

'The Garamantian government may have their own reasons for sending us an ungenuine exhibition. That is a matter I should have to take up with the Foreign Office. The insurance valuations were made in Tripoli, where Lloyd's men were certainly convinced they were seeing the real thing. Whether they really did, or whether what they saw was really flown over here, I cannot tell you. You remember that the Treasure was in any case only seriously insured against damage in transit. The replacement value was incalculable and had to be purely nominal, I think two or three million pounds.'

'Of course you'll contact the British Embassy in Garamantia?'

'A waste of time. Clearly they have slipped up already. That too will be a matter for investigation. The Chargé d'Affaires, by the way, is Pombo Greene, whom I have known, since he was in my election at Eton, to be exceptionally foolish and incompetent.'

'But the departments here . . .'

'Your department, Marcus, Funerary Art. You have the immediate responsibility for this Exhibition. It would have been perfectly possible for you to refuse that responsibility

– Egyptology was only too ready to take over – and so, with very little qualification, was Unglazed Ceramics – but, very naturally, you did not refuse. What did you yourself think of the grave-goods when they were unpacked?'

'I had never seen anything like them before,' replied Hawthorne-Mannering stiffly. 'I assumed that they had been provenanced. They are not in my field.'

'You had no suspicion at all of anything wrong?'

'I would have spoken at once . . .'

'Not necessarily. You're a secretive bastard, Marcus.'

'They are certainly gold,' said Hawthorne-Mannering. 'I can't be mistaken about that.'

'Certain areas are covered with gold leaf. Quite modern gold leaf. Untermensch had a sample of it in that case of his; I also sent down to conservation for a little book of it, and he showed me how it could be done.'

'What does he know about it?' Hawthorne-Mannering broke out with quite unaccustomed energy. 'Well, what does he? Isn't that the real point? Why should Untermensch know? He had never seen the Treasure, any more than the rest of us. He never had! That's what he came here to London for – to see it for the first time!'

'If my career has taught me anything,' said the Director, 'it is to recognise genuine knowledge and genuine expertise when I find them. I don't *know* that Untermensch is right; like every other scholar, he has had to study Garamantology at second hand. I can only say that after he had explained himself thoroughly, I felt that I could not usefully ignore his opinion. The incident has filled me, as it ought to have filled you, with profound doubt. We may be on the verge of a scandal which will destroy the credibility of the Museum, perhaps indeed of all museums, for ever.'

Hawthorne-Mannering appeared half suffocated, half weeping.

'Sir William! Of course, we can check the truth of all this at once. The only man outside Garamantia who can authenticate. We can ask Sir William! Ask him what he thinks!'

'It was exceedingly unfortunate that Sir William could not travel to Africa to supervise the whole operation. But his doctor's opinion was that the journey would kill him, and we know that since the material arrived he has – one supposes for sentimental reasons – refused to look at it.'

'He sent that man Jones down for something. That I know for a fact.'

'One or two of the clay tablets, I am informed. These, as I said, are genuine antiquities, but they are trash, simply thrown in by the Garamantian Minister of Information, Culture and Mental Hygiene as a makeweight.'

'Still, his objection to seeing the things can't be anything serious – you could show him the doll – you could set our minds at rest.'

'Sir William is my friend and benefactor,' said the Director slowly, 'and I believe, to some extent, respects my judgment. I should prefer him not to think me a fool. But that, in itself, hardly matters. I hesitate because of Sir William's known attitudes. I cannot altogether trust him, if the Treasure turns out to be a gigantic forgery, not to talk about it; he might even laugh. He is not, as I am, responsible to Trustees, two of whom are appointed by the Crown. He is not a museum man. He does not understand, as we do, what it means to have our good name and our dignity at stake.'

The Director's voice trembled with the pride and bitter jealousy which is the poetry of museum-keeping. As Hawthorne-Mannering immediately saw, he had reached the heart of the matter. But another agonising worry gripped him.

'Suppose one of the public notices!'

'I have sent down a message already, telling the staff, on the grounds of economy, to lower the lights.'

'And meanwhile, if Sir William won't do, we can, at least as far as the gold is concerned, call in someone, an Africanist, an Egyptologist, even a goldsmith or a working jeweller – Harari's of Coptic Street, he's a knowledgeable man.'

'And exactly what am I to ask him?'

'Well, one might say, do you think this gold is ancient, or a good replica – something of the kind. You could say it had been made by Technical Services. After all, the right to make copies is reserved to the Museum.'

'Should I not know, if it was made by one of our own departments, whether it was a replica or not?'

'Then perhaps one would have to speak more frankly – admit it was one of the exhibits, only that we had some reason to doubt.'

'And how am I to frame my request? "Could you kindly tell me whether this item, which is being shown every day to thousands of the paying public in the most famous museum in the world, which is illustrated in our catalogue and known to every schoolchild in the country, is in fact an ingenious imitation, knocked up in the Casbah?" '

'You could ask them to treat the matter in confidence. Well, more than that, some promise of secrecy . . .'

'And how long would that last? How long before a hint is dropped, and the media get to hear of it? Even in twenty or thirty years, only a word in some garrulous autobiography or memoir – where then would our reputation stand? You are a different case, Marcus; you will never be able to speak. Perhaps I may venture to remind you again that the Exhibition is ultimately your responsibility.'

It was not unkindly said, but Hawthorne-Mannering floundered and cringed.

'I have no idea, no idea at all, what is to be done.'

'You don't look altogether well. Are you all right?'

'One feels faint.'

The Director took out of a cupboard a bottle of Fino La Ina and poured out a large glassful for his subordinate. It was half-past nine in the morning.

'Do you often get spells of faintness?'

'No, no. A sometimes thing.'

Hawthorne-Mannering sipped delicately. The Director took nothing himself, but began to pace to and fro.

'We need a man of expert judgment who can be shown this object without being asked if it is genuine or not – simply as a matter of interest, so that his reactions may be noted. A connoisseur, who values artefacts only for their age and beauty.'

'Rochegrosse-Bergson? . . .'

'Bergson knows nothing, either about this or any other subject. Pull yourself together, Marcus.'

'I apologise. But if this man is to be a Garamantologist as well – wouldn't he be rather unusual?'

'Fortunately the Museum world is rich in unusual people. There is such a man. He has never published anything except a note or so in *Antiquitas*. Nevertheless he is probably, after Sir William himself and Untermensch, the world's leading Garamantologist. It has even been suggested – in complete secrecy, of course – that he has been allowed to see the Treasure itself, though that would be a political matter, somewhat outside my province.'

'Who is he? Where does he live?'

'His name is Semyonov – Professor Cyril Ivanovitch Semyonov. He is attached to the University of Moscow.'

'But why hasn't he visited the exhibition? There's been no Russian delegation at all . . .'

'They received an invitation in the ordinary way but did not send any official reply – I am told for purely diplomatic reasons. The United States, Cuba, France, Egypt and China are all negotiating for concessions to excavate in Garamantia. Russia, most uncharacteristically, although she is on excellent terms with the Garamantian Government, seems to have been excluded. A puzzling situation, perhaps taken as an insult. As to the loan of the Treasure itself . . .'

He paused. Hawthorne-Mannering had not been shown the Cabinet memoranda; there was no need to explain further.

'But is it possible to get in touch with this Semyonov?'

'Certainly. In fact, I have had considerable correspondence with him.'

'But I've never even heard of him! I thought copies of all relevant correspondence were to be passed to my office!'

The Director dismissed this with a slight gesture.

'And in any case if he's not going to come here . . .'

'He is not going to come to London. There is nothing, as far as I know, to prevent one of our staff going to visit him in Moscow.'

'With the doll.'

'With the doll.'

'Is this . . . may one ask . . . is this what you have been thinking of doing all along?'

'It is a somewhat desperate solution. I sent for you because I thought you might have some other idea to offer. But if we are to do it this way, it must be done at once, and quite unofficially. It must seem almost casual. No notification to the Cultural Attaché in Moscow, or any nonsense of that kind. Someone quite junior must be sent, of no particular importance, and he need be told very little about it. He should go over tomorrow, I think as an ordinary tourist on a package weekend. That will probably mean going to Leningrad first, but that only wastes a couple of days. All he has to do, when he reaches Moscow, is to contact Semyonov. He should, if possible, know a little Russian, not too much, enough for a short explanation – show him the doll and carefully note his reactions. It will be obvious at once from the professor's manner whether he regards it as the priceless original or simply an ingenious imitation.'

'But what kind of explanation would he give?'

'A sort of courtesy visit. Since Semyonov was unavoidably prevented from coming here. He'll have to learn the Russian for "unavoidably prevented".'

'But won't this Professor think it rather strange that a junior official should be allowed to fly out with an object of such value?'

'Not if he is as he appears in his letters, and as he has been described to me. He lives from day to day, careless of protocol, and dreaming of the artisans of the first millennium. And when you say "an object of such value" . . .'

Hawthorne-Mannering shuddered.

'Quite. But still, if it is a replica – if it turns out to be of no value at all – how can one be sure that Semyonov won't talk about it? He can give us away as easily as anyone else.'

As usual when he was nervously excited he was choosing his words less carefully. 'Give us away' was far too crude. The Director, however, chose to overlook it.

'Semyonov has the reputation of being exceedingly absentminded.'

'Like Sir William?'

'I think in quite a different way. Sir William, under his vagueness, is still a very shrewd old fellow. Semyonov is said to be a kind of caricature, living in a mental haze of past civilisations. Everyday matters simply pass him by. There are jokes about him, one hears, in the Moscow Circus.'

'What were his letters like?'

'Almost unintelligible, except when he came to details of Garamantology. Then, the translators informed me, they were as clear as crystal.'

Hawthorne-Mannering was recovering. His bird-like face, already delicately flushed by the sherry, brightened perceptibly.

'You say a junior official, no one important? Perhaps one could contribute a thought . . . There is a young, quite young Exhibition officer, an AP3 . . .'

'Yes, I know who you mean. He did the catalogue for you, the last time or the last time but one you went on sick leave.'

'On that occasion he very much exceeded his duties. The catalogue could very well have been left till I returned. However, Smith does know a little Russian. I believe he took advantage of the Museum's extension course in Modern Languages last year which, I fear, was not attended by many of the personnel.'

'Is he intelligent?'

'Sufficiently, I daresay.'

'Well, if the doll turns out to be a replica, we shall simply have to tell him of course it was – we couldn't have entrusted the original to an AP3. If Semyonov is overcome with excitement, delight, recognition and so forth, then of course we shall have to tell Smith – is he called that? it sounds manageable enough – we shall have to point out to him that he has been greatly honoured in being asked to act as our official courier, and we must see to it that he doesn't get above himself.'

Hawthorne-Mannering's expression somewhat resembled a smile. The Director interpreted the expression as relief and thought he understood it well enough. Here, however, he misjudged considerably. In fact, Hawthorne-Mannering thought the whole scheme absolute madness, an index of how deeply Sir John must be disturbed, and he devoutly believed that it must end in the discredit of Waring Smith. He might well be arrested in Moscow. One often was. The Director, too, might find it necessary to resign, and then the whole hierarchy of the Museum might – though it was not a certainty – move one place up.

'A certain degree of intelligence, then,' the Director went on. 'The Doll, of course, must not be declared at the customs, either going in or out. That is an advantage of the package tours, on which, I am informed by those who know about them, the luggage is only superficially examined.'

Hawthorne-Mannering looked at his overlord with renewed respect. To have so much knowledge on subjects so obscure!

'Waring Smith would do, I am certain,' he repeated.

'Make the arrangements, then, Marcus. I shall see him tomorrow, before he goes. And tell Miss Rank to make it as early as possible.'

Responsive to the tone of authority, Hawthorne-Mannering glided out. The Director made a note in his private diary. 'H-M perhaps a good deal stronger character than he looks. "The only emperor is the emperor of ice-cream." '

Waring Smith stood with thirty compatriots, their luggage labelled conspicuously as in the charge of Suntreader Holidays, on the open platform of the Leningrad Station in Moscow, looking out into the bleakness of Komsomol-skaya square.

He was shivering in the faint haze of powder snow, which was gradually covering the waiting, stamping passengers and the piles of luggage with a thin veil of white. They had been temporarily abandoned by the lady representative of In-tourist, who had told them on no account to move from the platform until she came back to fetch them to their hotel.

Waring was quite inadequately dressed for the weather. Every other member of the party seemed to possess long leather or sheepskin coats, acquired on previous package tours to Asia Minor, and everyone else had gone, during the two days they had just spent in Leningrad, to the berioska shop, and had bought themselves a large fur hat with ear-flaps. Their appearance was that of a mingled flock of docile hairy animals, dating from some era in the dawn of history when nomad man herded many species together. Waring had come in an Aran sweater, not very successfully knitted by Haggie, and his winter raincoat. Haggie had also done him a scarf, and this effectively hid the swollen mark round his neck, which was better, but only somewhat better, since Monday.

Waring's instructions themselves had been few, but rather beyond his comprehension. Two days in Leningrad: then on to Moscow where he had to carry out his commission. Ring Professor Semyonov – the number, which he knew by heart, was 36-94-43 – ask when it would be convenient to call, a courtesy visit, nothing official, the Treasure not likely to be shown again in the near future, perhaps Professor Semyonov would care to see etc. etc. When he got back,

Waring would be expected to give an account of the interview immediately, simply for the record; he was rather fortunate, as no doubt he realised, to be taking a break in the middle of the exacting period of the Exhibition, when all the personnel were working at full stretch. It was just – though this was implied rather than put into words – that he was junior enough to be spared quite easily, and the whole matter, after all, was a politeness to a foreign scholar, but not of great importance.

Waring had not questioned this, and harassed by his loneliness at home – Haggie had not sent on her new address – he had rather looked forward to going to the USSR for the first time.

His travel arrangements had been made personally by Miss Rank, who had probably never booked a package tour in her life before, and Waring felt a strong urge to apologise as she coldly handed him his bright pink ticket-folder, labels and tags. He had been allowed to say where he was going, though not what he was doing, and he had received very little by way of farewell. Dousha was on sick-leave – she was said to have violent indigestion – and Sir William, though he sent a kind word, was unfortunately too busy to see him.

Jones, in his usual grizzled and grizzling way, had issued a general warning that things would probably be worse by the time he came back. 'By the way,' he added, 'I found out who took them keys the other night.'

'Who?'

'Mr Coker.'

'Did he say anything?'

'He wasn't there. I was just looking round like I do and I saw them in his drawing office.'

'What did you do with them?'

'Straight back to Sir William, of course.'

'But Len Coker's all right. I still believe he's all right.'

'That I can't say. But I know he's rather too fond of taking things that don't belong to him.'

With Len himself Waring had naturally felt exceedingly

awkward. He had seen him for a moment sitting in the cafeteria, his stocky figure suggesting, in every sense of the word, solidarity. But there was so much, like the result of the last few days, that couldn't be mentioned between them. Cannabis, fish-spears, unexplained throttling, keys, and then Waring's own expedition, which, however unimportant, was certainly strictly confidential.

'So you don't want to tell me,' said Len. 'You stick to it that you're just going on holiday. It doesn't make a blind bit of difference. I don't know why you're going and I don't care. But I've no objection to saying that I'll miss you.'

Waring felt then, and still felt standing on the Moscow platform in the snow, that whatever might or might not have happened, he could have done with Len's company.

The train journey from Leningrad, in a compartment specially reserved for Suntreaders, had been a curious experience. Outside the windows were the interminable fields, sometimes blankly white, sometimes with rye straw poking up above the snow and caught by the lights of the train; at long intervals came houses and villages adrift, or a solitary figure battling its way to an outhouse at the back of nowhere. Inside the carriage, the Suntreaders drew together over their numerous shopping bags – they were now more like pack animals than a pastoral flock. During the two days in Leningrad Waring had been a not unwelcome member of the group. His inadequate raincoat had made them pity him. Now, his halting Russian, produced for the first time, to speak to the train attendant, made them hate him, as having an unfair advantage. When the train drew into the Leningrad station at half-past two in the morning, Waring felt almost wholly isolated.

Even more troubling was a very strong illusion – it must, of course, be that – that he was being watched, or even, perhaps, followed. This idea, or rather the idea that he could have such an idea, was so irritating to Waring that he almost forgot the discomfort of his sore neck and frozen feet. How old was he, after all? Being 'followed' by a mysterious stranger had been his preoccupation thirteen years ago, when he pored over the pages of the *Dandy* and the *Beezer*. It was ludicrous. If by any chance the Soviet authorities knew about the golden toy in his hand-luggage and wanted to have a look at it, they only had to stop him at the customs, or indeed anywhere else, or give a hint to the Intourist lady. That he was a Museum official they could tell from his passport and visa, and as to the secret report on the organisation of the Exhibition, if Waring knew what was in it, so, quite certainly, did they. There was nothing in what he was doing that could possibly make him an object of suspicion.

Nevertheless he had repeatedly seen in Leningrad a small figure in a long dark overcoat, not a Russian one, and a black fur cap with the ear-flaps pulled down, like a child or a foreigner. Well, how often had he seen him? At least four times, quite enough to begin to wonder uneasily when he would see him next. He was never directly behind Waring, always a little in front, a few places ahead in the endless cloakroom queue at the Hermitage, disappearing round a corner, in a flurry of driven snow, under the three-globed street lamps of Leningrad. He seemed indeed to belong to Leningrad. It was most unlikely that he would be on the train. But when Waring had negotiated his way to the buffet car, he had seen there, as always with his back to him, bent over a glass of tea, the insignificant man in the dark overcoat.

Waring believed that he might be able to clear his mind of absurdities if he were not on the verge of frost-bite. He concentrated unwillingly, as a counter-irritant, on the subject of his debt to the Whitstable and Protective Building Society. The relief, ten minutes later, of being transferred to the heated Intourist bus was so great that, with his eyes and nose melted into lukewarm tears, he was unable to feel any emotion but senseless gratitude. Now, in the vast reception area of the Hotel Zolotoy, much bigger than that of the Museum, his wits returned to him.

Crowded into a carved and gilded lift with two family parties of Suntreaders, he ground up to the twelfth floor. There the *klyuchnitza*, or key-lady, imperturbably knitting, sat presiding over the corridor with her altar-like desk of keys. A little grand-daughter, with two fair pigtails sticking out each side of her round head, stood by her side, holding the skein of wool, and stared unwinkingly at the uncouth visitors.

Waring – Nomer 1217 – was the odd man out. In a sense he was lucky, since there was no other unattached male on the trip, and in Moscow, as in Leningrad, he had a double room to himself. 1217 was a heated box, like hotel rooms all over the world. He sat down, took off his shoes, and thought of Haggie; he asked himself how much longer he would have to go on sleeping alone. Tomorrow, what was more, he would have to make contact with Semyonov; the real job of work would begin. Nothing, really, to worry about there, but he wished he was still in Leningrad and that the view from the window was still the wonderful expanse of the Neva under ice, filling the room with reflected ice-light. Instead of that he could just make out, beyond a kind of well of dense Thibetan darkness, the corner of Red Square. The stars on the Kremlin were hidden, but he could see their brilliant red glow which they cast into the tremulous frosty air.

Without any warning or any introductory knock, the little girl with fair pigtails walked into the middle of the room and stood there, with her small calves in woollen stockings pressed closely together.

'Tchoongoom!'

Waring liked children and was not at all sorry to have her company, but he simply did not know what she meant.

'Tchoongoom!'

It was absurd to start looking up words in a dictionary to understand a little girl of, perhaps, six. GUM, of course, was the department store in Red Square. Then it came to him. Chewing-gum! It was the one great shortage in the USSR, the one commodity for which the Russians still envied the West. And he had brought none with him, not a single packet.

It was a shame to disappoint her. Perhaps he had something else she would like. On an impulse he opened his suitcase and took out the doll, once, after all, the favourite companion, in life and death, of the Golden Child. The key-lady's grand-daughter watched carefully as he took it out of the Museum packaging. As first the face, and then the hands, emerged, her own expression of angelic firmness seemed to crumple up, and with eyes full of tears she roared.

'Nekulturnye!'

Not nice! Not civilised! The treasured toy, brought half-way across the world to show to the appreciative eyes of scholarship, was utterly rejected. As a toy, it clearly was one of the great failures of history. And really, Waring thought, it was not very nice, and not civilised. Had the Golden Child really liked it? The little girl fled bellowing from his room.

Early as he was next morning, he found all the Suntreaders already at table.

'I suppose we shan't have the pleasure of your company on today's itinerary, Mr Smith.'

Waring didn't know why they should suppose this. He wondered how they knew his name: he didn't know any of theirs. What was the itinerary? It turned out to be Orientation, with a visit to the Pushkin Museum of Fine Arts and an Opportunity for Shopping in the morning; lunch; afternoon coach visit to the Park and Exhibition of Economic Achievement, with optional troika ride (extra); evening, *Giselle* at the New Kremlin Theatre (third company and understudies), meet at the Spasskaya Gate – only everybody's tickets had already been given out, so Waring would have to take the alternative, marking him out as an unsuccessful Suntreader – the State Circus on Tsvetnoy Boulevard.

'But that will be quite good too,' they told him, 'you will see Splitov the clown.'

Attendants suddenly brought the whole breakfast for everybody, all at once. It had not been asked for, and its arrival was entirely arbitrary. Heavy cutlery, suitable for a boyar, thundered on to the table. Before the queasy Suntreaders were placed large dishes of ham, seethed onions, fiercely pickled cucumbers and mushrooms, raw beef, mountains of butter, black, white and grey bread, cheese, piroshki, caviare pancakes and unidentifiable fried objects. Samovars and large kettles were wheeled up and streams of tea shot accurately over the shoulders of the guests into thick white cups, while more samovars were banged down on the overloaded table, which, though strong, rocked dangerously. Waring, as a displaced rye loaf fell on to his lap, was considering how early he could ring up Semyonov. Perhaps now, before the morning coach went off to the Pushkin.

The telephone call was unexpectedly successful. A voice answered from 36-94-43 – a middle-aged woman's voice, interrupted with bursts of shrill laughter. These, perhaps, were the result of shyness. Certainly, certainly, this was the home of Professor Semyonov. He was not there at the moment, he was taking a walk. Yes, he took a walk every, every morning (screams of laughter). This was his sister-in-law speaking. The name of the Museum was instantly recognised, and another woman's voice, somewhat younger, took over to assure the honoured caller that he would be welcome at any time. 'I'll get it over,' thought Waring, and asked if he could come to see them that morning, about eleven. He had missed the Suntreaders' coach anyway; he had seen it through the window, pulling out from the many others parked outside the hotel, 'Yes, yes! this very morning!' The address was 35 Leo-Tolstova, yes, yes, Tolstoy street, and it would be very agreeable. Something to show

77

to the Professor, to Cyril Ivanovitch? That would be even much more agreeable still!

Waring had not met with such approval for anything he had done for quite a long time. He thanked the desk clerk who had got the number for him, and was not allowed to receive gratuities, but breathed a request for tchoongoom; I'll never come to this country again without a dozen packets of spearmint, Waring thought. Suppose Semyonov's sister-in-law asks for some?

The air outside the revolving doors pierced his lungs like a crystal knife. It was as though he had never been quite awake before. The wind seemed to come in several directions at once, whirling the snowdust round the corners of the sidestreets. It was very much colder than in Leningrad. How many degrees of frost?

Rounding the corner of the Kremlin across Manezhnaya Square, with a doubtful glance at the severe façade of the Arsenal, he came on a sight which almost made him feel that he had never left the Museum. It was the queue – not the shorter tourists's queue, but the people's queue – to see the mummy of Lenin. Twice round the frozen Alexandrov-skaya Gardens, up Manezhnaya and into Red Square, the patient files stood black against the snow. The park statues were covered with shrouds of straw to protect them against the cold, but the human beings stood there, wiping the frozen drops from noses and eyelashes, waiting with im-memorial patience to see what they had been told was worth seeing. In an hour and a half they would be filing past the embalmed head and hands, and the ghastly evening dress suit, of Lenin. Sentries would hiss at them so that they would go past in perfect silence, and they would emerge after thirty seconds, having seen what they had waited for, perhaps for years.

Keeping the river on his left, still skirting the snow-bound towers and bridges of the Kremlin, Waring crossed into Kropotkinskaya and at the same time, entered Moscow's past. Leo Tolstova was quite deserted, no traffic, no passers-by. What could be more appropriate to the scholar whom he was going to visit than this street in which Tolstoy himself had lived at no. 21, a street of wooden balconies and birch trees where the morning snow had not even now been brushed away from the steps?

No. 35, however, turned out to be quite unlike the rest of the street. It was a small block of flats, probably built about ten years ago, and of relentlessly dull appearance. There were no lifts; a narrow moving staircase, out of order at the moment, was supposed to take the tenants and their shopping from floor to floor. The hall was decorated with unpleasant mosaics in honour of Chernishevsky, chipped, and missing a number of bits of marble. The name-board had very few cards in it. Waring was relieved to see one – faded and yellowed, it was true – bearing the name Cyril Ivanovitch Semyonov. He toiled up to the fourth floor, duffle-bag in his hand, and in it, as he was constantly and almost guiltily aware, the golden Weeping Doll. For the first time he began to worry not only about the oddness of his mission, but the oddness of Semyonov. The unprepossessing block of flats, a very long way, when you came to think of it, from the University district, suggested that he might be in disgrace, perhaps somewhere in that area where political disfavour and academic jealousy met. If he had not come to England, perhaps it was because he had not been allowed to. On the other hand, there seemed to be no objection at all to his receiving a visit from a representative of the Museum. There *seemed* not to be. Waring wished he could be absolutely sure of this point. I'm out of my depth, he thought. Get it over.

A ring on the bell produced a long wait. Then a kind of grating in the front door was pushed aside, and a sharp eye and half a nose appeared. Waring explained his mission once again. He had an appointment, he had telephoned an hour ago.

'You want to see Cyril Ivanovitch?'

'Yes. Perhaps you are his sister-in-law?'

'He has no sister-in-law.'

Waring was not sure he had got the word right – *nevestka*. Still, it was always possible to make a mistake.

'I'm sorry . . . perhaps his sister?'

'Cyril Ivanovitch has no sister.'

Waring thought fleetingly of Dousha, to whom this kind of oblique conversation came so naturally.

'I was told I might come at eleven o'clock. I have an important message for Professor Semyonov – well, quite important.'

'Yes, that is right, quite right. Unfortunately he is in the country.'

'I was told he'd gone for a walk!'

'Yes, that is so, a walk in the country.'

'When will he be back?'

There were certainly other women in the flat. He could hear them talking and clattering in the background.

'Would it be more convenient if I called tomorrow? I am only in Moscow for two days. But I could come at the same time tomorrow, at eleven o'clock. Would the professor be back from the country then?'

No laughter now, and no welcome. But at least he obtained another appointment. Tomorrow at eleven, that was understood.

'But Professor Semyonov will be here?' he pleaded.

'Why not?'

The grille closed, and Waring turned away in bewilderment with his laden duffle-bag. He would rejoin the Suntreaders, he thought, for the afternoon expedition. They might not receive him enthusiastically, but they could not quite reject him, and it would be better than facing the rest of the day by himself. And his instructions, after all, were to appear as much as possible like an ordinary tourist. It was a kind of reassurance to find them at table, mollified by the morning's shopping which lay heaped around them. Waring, stumbling over a gaily painted zither, was immediately fastened upon, the only one who had not been to the Pushkin, to be told how much he had missed. At least I'm a bit of use to them in that way, he thought.

But it was a relief when, at the Park of Economic Achievements, a vast wintry steppe lying off the Mira Prospect, the whole of the party deserted him to queue for a troika ride. It was a matter of choice, and Waring very much wanted to see the Space Pavilion. Here, after a walk of nearly a mile over the snow-bound plateau, he found himself almost alone. The huge Space Hall, perhaps with some idea of realism, was unheated, and the cold was intense beyond the imagination of Siberia. Every other pavilion glowed with central heating, and all, even the Achievements of Sub-Regional State Electrification, were packed to capacity with warm, gaping or dozing visitors, whose thousand faces could be seen through the steaming glass. Waring, unable to feel his feet or the tips of his ears, but with a spirit not unworthy of the astronauts themselves, forged grimly onwards until he was satisfied that he had seen, probably for the only time in his life, every one of the twenty-two lunar projects.

Afraid of missing the coach again, and of appearing standoffish, he took a seat in the Exhibition electric tramway which clanged and banged, open to every wind that blew, through the icy wastes surrounding the Regional Pavilions to the Triumphal entrance gate. The tramway did not seem to be popular, or perhaps this was not a popular time to take it. The only other occupant was sitting two carriages in front. You could see him quite clearly, if you wanted to, as the tram swung violently round the bends of its zig-zag course. He was a small man who sat quietly by himself, without turning round, in a black coat.

'Shall I simply go up to him when this thing stops?' Waring asked himself. 'Shall I stand in front of him and say: "This is not 1935. Britain, much though I love my country, cannot be considered, even by courtesy, as anything but a second-class power, and I am not a representative even of my department in the museum. Perhaps you think I'm someone else – I'm perfectly normal, and ordinary, I'm prepared to admit that I probably look like someone else. If not, why are you" – he couldn't say following – "why are you always going in front of me?".' He wished he had brought his Russian dictionary, the last bit might be rather difficult to express. But when the tramway reached the entrance – it did not stop, only slowed down, and you made a jump for it – Waring, as he landed cautiously on the slippery path, saw that the black-coated man had not got out, but was carried away forward, bumping and swaying, apparently in a never-ending round of Economic Achievements.

The coach was gone after all, and Waring, after buying himself a dumpling at the untidy peasant market just outside the gates, plunged thankfully into the Vistavska metro station. He was conveyed back, through the marble and gilded halls of the deep-level stations, to the centre of Moscow.

By four o'clock darkness had begun to set in, creeping across a pale pure green sky. By six, Moscow prepared, with sluggish and secretive power, to enjoy itself for the evening. Waring stood, with many others, reading the spread-out pages of today's *Pravda*, which were exhibited under glass for those who had not managed, or could not afford, to buy a copy. There was a small crowd looking at the headlines and the cartoons, and Waring was left with the domestic correspondence page. Strangely enough, the same theme, the same preoccupation: letter after letter complained about the queueing and overcrowding which disgraced the People's cultural recreations. Six hours' wait for the Lenin Mausoleum, three or four for the Pushkin. Comrades must wait another eternity to get back their hats and coats which were compulsorily deposited; their feet were trampled, ribs broken. In Lenin's words, what was to be done?

The service that evening was capriciously slow, and as the Suntreaders would not have dreamed of departing without their dinner, everyone was late for the evening entertainment. The ballet group, although the Kremlin was only two hundred yards away, were conveyed by coach; the circusgoers set off through the thickening snow to catch Tram 15, 18 or 20.

They arrived towards the end of the first part. The scene, as they struggled into their seats high above the arena, struck Waring as more like an execution than a circus. No one was either smiling or laughing. The musicians were silent. The children stared unblinkingly, as the key-lady's grandchild had done, at the brilliantly lighted ring.

The act, or number, represented a village fair, presumably, from the boots and embroidered costumes, in Georgia. The sanded arena swarmed with girls pretending to sell bottles of wine and brightly painted toys. Live hens were running about; one of them got into the audience, and was caught by an attendant, who wrung its neck. In the midst of the turmoil, the reassuringly red-nosed figure of the clown Splitov controlled the scene with a few gestures of his huge white-gloved hands.

At his command the brass band struck up Khachaturian's *Sabre Dance*, and a team of shaggy horses cantered in, dragging a *telyega* out of which stepped the scarecrow figure of a village priest, accompanied by his sacristan. Both these clerical figures wore crosses and long grey beards, which might have come out of a Christmas cracker. The peasants bowed low as they advanced towards a steaming pot on one of the stalls, dipped their fingers in and licked them, and then, seizing two property ladles, began to eat greedily. The swallowing, smacking and belching echoed through the amplification into a monstrous din. A kiss which sounded like high-powered suction machinery indicated that the clerics had started in on the Georgian girls. But both this and the music were drowned by an even louder bellow.

'Beware, comrades! They will take all that you have! Do not listen to them! Listen, instead, to the wisdom of Splitov!'

The great clown advanced with two nooses of rope and, to mild applause, threw them over the necks of the priest and sacristan. There was a roll of drums, a moment of darkness. Then in the dazzling spot-lights high, immensely high among the steel girders, could be seen the two dangling figures in beards and black cassocks, their heads lolling sideways.

To the rhythm of a jolly folk tune the performers were running round the ring and making for the exits. Some of them tumbled and turned somersaults. What a mixture of costumes there was! And some of them looked rather old to be in a circus, even a state circus. One of them was wearing what was certainly a clown's head-dress, something like a chicken's beak, but underneath that he had on a long dark overcoat. Waring reproved himself for the cold shock he felt. This was mania. He was not mistaken, though. He knew that coat.

'*Nomer* 1217,' he said to the *klyuchnitza*, who, as before, was on night duty. Did the little grand-daughter never go to bed? She stood firmly by the desk, one hand on her granny's lap, meeting Waring's look with her round blue stare. He could only hope that she hadn't denounced him as the nasty tourist who had frightened her with an uncultivated dolly.

'Please, *nomer* 1217,' he repeated.

The *klyuchnitza* shook her head. 'That is not your *nomer*.'

'But it is! 1217! It's the one you gave me! I slept in it last night, all my things are there!'

'No. It is a mistake. For you there is no *nomer* on this floor.'

The little girl's stare took on a tinge of reproof. The *klyuchnitza* folded her arms, and then somewhat insultingly – for Waring's Russian had served him quite well all day – went to fetch the floor interpreter. She was a Georgian, amply built, not unlike an older version of Dousha.

'Ah yes, what is the trouble? You have been to the State Circus. That is so exciting. You have been too much excited by the Clown Splitov?'

84

'I'm not in the least excited,' said Waring. 'I'd like to be allowed into my room, though, and to go to bed.'

'Ah, to bed!' cried the interpreter gaily, 'but you are not now on the right floor! Your room is upstairs.'

On the top floor, at an unimaginable height, Waring, toiling after her flouncing steps, was shown into what apparently was now his room. The sight of it made him gasp. Thickly carpeted in crimson, shining with crystal, draped with lace, it seemed to have been prepared for some Tsarevitch who had escaped the final massacre. Polished wooden stands for suits, for shoes, for uniforms, stood in rows like the trees of the forest. The fine marble mantelshelf was crowded with Fabergé figures of gypsy singers, executed in coloured stones. On one of the damask walls, incongruously framed in gold, hung a sketch by Repin for the *Volga Boatmen*. On the table waiting in an ornamental wine-cooler, was a sizeable bottle of the unpleasant Russian champagne.

'But this can't be for me,' Waring stammered, 'it's an error – *ashipka* – a complete mistake. I'm on a package tour – a Suntreader All-in Winter Breakaway. This room has to belong to someone else. Not me, it can't be for me. Who does it belong to anyway?'

'It belongs to the People,' replied the interpreter.

'Then what am I doing here?'

'The People wish you to sleep here. Spakoenoye noche! Peaceful nights!'

On Sunday, Professor Semyonov was still not at home.

Waring thought he might write this down as possibly the most unsuccessful Sunday he had ever spent. Romanov for a night, he had slept well, and he could not pretend that he hadn't appreciated the splendour as he ascended the three mahogany steps to the bath and turned the gold-plated taps from which rusty hot water gushed forth. But these moments were obliterated by the difficulty of carrying out his mission, the nagging worry that if he left the imperial quarters, even for a few hours, he might never get back again – he had not been given a key – and the yet more urgent necessity to conceal his change of room from the Suntreaders, who would resent it exceedingly. Much of their spare time was taken up with complaining that their accommodation was not what they had been promised, that they had no view of the Kremlin and that no water came out of the taps.

Waring had avoided them and gone straight to Red Square to see what he could buy at GUM, but he had patrolled the gaunt bazaars and galleries in vain, searching for a suitable offering for Haggie. Then, at 35 Leo-Tolstova, he had met a total blank. It was not simply that Semyonov was still away. Everybody might be away. The grille in the door did not open when he rang the bell. He rang again and again. There was no answer; nobody came at all. Finally a half-interested, half-grumbling neighbour, half in pyjamas and half in tram-conductor's uniform, appeared from the flat opposite. It was no good ringing, the family were not there, they had gone for a walk. 'When would they be back?' The neighbour was unable to say. 'Where did he think they were walking?' 'In the country. Where else could one walk?'

Waring did not feel that he would be ashamed to go back to London and report on what he had not managed to do. He had not asked for this job, and he had carried out his instructions as far as he could. The possibility that Semyonov might not be in Moscow at all had apparently not occurred to anyone. Nevertheless dissatisfaction from some source too murky to identify began to flood over him as he walked. The suddenness of the whole assignment – the Director had spoken of it almost as a kind of privilege – the disapproving little girl, the laughing woman on the telephone, the frustrated visits to Semyonov, the disappearing room, the man in the dark overcoat – a needless mystery that began and ended nowhere! And even before that, the sickening moment when he had been half strangled in the night, the odd remarks of Jones, the odder behaviour of Len. Why couldn't these people, why couldn't everyone, be reasonable, or at least intelligible? Was that too much to ask? He didn't feel that he had been tried and found wanting, rather that he had not been tried and had no idea whether he was wanting or not.

The snow had stopped falling; the cold hung in the air like white smoke. He began to walk again, without any fixed destination. A sensation of warmth, coming from a grating in the pavement, told him he was passing a *stolovaya*, a low-price dining-room. Might as well unfreeze my feet for ten minutes, he thought. He pushed his way through the glass door, shoved his way downstairs, and, as the law required, deposited his raincoat at the counter just inside.

'Your case too, Comrade Tourist! You must deposit your case!'

Waring never did this, as it contained the golden doll. Fortunately the crush in the passage was so intense, with workers and diners trying to go both in and out and to give in and take back piles of hats and overcoats, that he was able to squeeze past unnoticed.

The *stolovaya* was in a humid basement which must have survived several eras of planned building. Waring put down his kopeks for a glass of tea and took his place at a plastic-covered table. He was no one and knew nobody. It was a moment of melancholy peace. Then, looking up, he saw through the window on to the street, which was high enough up to be almost clear of steam, the familiar figure of the man in the dark overcoat.

'That's the first time he's ever been behind me,' Waring thought. 'He's coming in here. We're going to meet.' It occurred to him, also, that the man was not exactly a stranger. He did not know him, but he had seen him somewhere before, not in Russia, and not very long ago either.

The chair opposite him, which had remained empty, was pulled back. Someone else who had refused to give up his case! Not a suitcase, though, but an excessively shabby briefcase. The stranger put it carefully under the table before he sat down.

'Professor Untermensch!'

'Of course, who else?'

Waring was entirely taken aback.

'Mr Smith, I think I last had the pleasure of seeing you at the Museum when you brought one of the grave-goods of the Golden Child to the Director's room, that he might show it to me.'

Professor Untermensch was one of the world's leading authorities on the Garamantian script. You couldn't ask him whether he had been running round the circus ring last night, wearing a hat like the beak of a chicken.

'You may say that we have never been formally introduced,' Untermensch went on, 'but since we are both now here, let us follow the Russian custom, and embrace each other!'

To Waring's amazement he actually did this, leaning over the plastic table-cloth, and kissing him first on one cheek, then on the other. Waring had never really got the hang of doing this. He moved his nose the wrong way, and his cheek was abraded by the rim of the Professor's spectacles.

'Well, well, we are lucky to have this freeze,' said Untermensch, settling back in his chair. 'The freeze, which destroys the germs of infection, becomes rarer and rarer, so it is said, in big cities. The breath of so many millions, the central heating – where can the frost get its grip? But this winter we see the Moscow of a thousand snows – the cold that defeated Buonaparte!'

He noisily swallowed a spoonful of cabbage soup.

'Look here,' said Waring. 'You are a scholar – an eminent scholar. I am a totally unimportant Exhibition Officer on a package week-end in Moscow. We are both sitting here in a workmen's diner. Have we really come here to talk about the weather?'

In completely fluent Russian, the Professor begged one of his neighbours to give him the pepper, and poured it liberally into his soup-bowl.

'You know you've been following me,' said Waring

desperately. 'I've caught sight of you everywhere. I can't have been mistaken. You're supposed to be in London. You can't be here. Why are you in Moscow?'

'I came because you came,' Untermensch replied. 'I wanted to see you.'

'But how the hell did you know I was here?'

Waring was not sure how polite he was supposed to be. The thickened air, heavy with the steam of vinegar, seemed to impede the course of his thoughts.

'How did I know you were here? That was not very difficult. I called up your department, and was told where you had gone. I was surprised, because on the continent very few museums give leave to the junior staff during exhibitions of this magnitude. I, however, know very little of English museum practice.'

'But you wanted to see me. Why?' asked Waring. The sense of unease, the familiar feeling, laid hold of him. The *stolovaya* was filling up with workmen, who had to deposit baskets of tools as well as many layers of outer garments.

'Why? Well, there were reasons. As poor Heine said – *es hat seine Gründe!* But perhaps I have not been quite accurate. I have not come to Moscow to see you. I have come to see what you have come to see.'

Waring could never be sure, either then or later, how long the two of them stayed in the *stolovaya*. What he did remember was that the Professor, with kindly hospitality, and perhaps moved by his young companion's bewildered state, had gone back to the queue at the counter and returned with a bottle of vodka. The *stolovaya* only stocked Narodnaya, the people's vodka, of a particularly cheap and fiery kind.

Waring never drank a great deal – Haggie did not much approve of it – and he did not drink a great deal now – just one or two glasses, which had the curious effect of submerging his intense desire to know what Untermensch was talking about, and let other worries float their way to the surface. Other worries, but also a golden glow of well-being so diffused that he did not even notice the moment when Untermensch, having won considerable popularity by offering the bottle to all the other diners within a wide area, slipped unobtrusively from the room.

Waring found himself alone, but no longer depressed. What was more, he knew perfectly well, as he collected raincoat and scarf, where he ought to be going next. At five o'clock, just about now, he was due at one of the sessions of the Dom Druzhba, at 16 Kalinin Street. This was the House of Friendship, run by the Union of Societies for Cultural Relations with Foreign Countries. Here visitors could, if they wished, ask questions about the Soviet regime, and would receive frank replies from representatives of the Ministry of Information. The Suntreaders had expressed some desire to attend, and if they were there it would be an opportunity to rejoin the group. He didn't feel that he minded them, or that he would mind them, nearly so much. After all, there was nothing wrong with a glass or two of spirits. It was largely a matter of habit. He still felt the central fire of the vodka warming his body and mind and gradually radiating outwards to the tip of his nose, which must be as red as the clown Splitov's. He could not tell whether he felt sad or happy, even at the memory of Haggie. He simply walked, hardly noticing that he had done so, back through Arbat Square and then to the right, up Kalinin Street.

No. 16, the House of Friendship, could not have been missed even after many glasses of vodka. It had been built by a wealthy merchant family, the Morozovs, who had decorated it with turrets and shells in the Portuguese Moorish style, giving it an unseemly air of rakish fantasy, not quite appropriate to the handing out of accurate information.

The frozen steps were difficult to negotiate, but the tipsy Waring Smith felt come over him a new mood, one of vast and irrational irritation. Its origins lay in the past, long before his visit to the Soviet Union, perhaps in the Museum, perhaps with the mortgage company, but wherever it came from, and he did not ever remember feeling quite like this before, the effect was overwhelming. He felt driven up the wooden staircase, past the attendant who shouted out to him to deposit his coat, into the reception chamber where every head was turned as he burst in. On the platform, two officials in sober blue suits were seated in attitudes of quiet attention, while in the body of the hall one of the Suntreaders had just put up her hand, and, with a Women's Institute diary open before her, was just about to put a question.

'I want to know something,' shouted Waring. 'I'm going to have an answer, even though I'm arrested as a trouble maker and thrown out of the mortgage tour and the package company lock me in the Lubyanka. I didn't come here to come here! I came here to talk to Semyonov, that one bloody thing, and you're all going to take a walk in the country and tell me where he bloody is! That! Where he is! What's become of Semyonov!'

He jumped across an empty bench and ran towards the platform. Though the hall seethed, the officials sat smiling imperturbably. Controlling hands moved him without violence through a side entrance. Where was Semyonov? He struggled, imploring them to tell him. The stairs were slipping away downwards beneath his feet. The air was bitter cold again. He was being invited firmly to enter a large black car, a Zil, waiting in a no-parking area in Kalinin Street.

Waring had just reached the stage of hoping that the vodka was not wearing off, since at that point he would certainly have to have some sort of reckoning with himself. His mind shied away. He was a British citizen. You couldn't be arrested for asking the whereabouts of a respected Professor of Moscow University, even if rather emphatically. You couldn't – could you? – be arrested for taking a glass or two of vodka. It was a good thing he hadn't deposited his overcoat, anyway, or he wouldn't have had time to get it back. That was something.

They were going to the Kremlin. The Zil drove straight across the Trinity Bridge and through the Trinity Gate into the Kremlin. This was not the ordinary tourist entrance. There were guards who saluted. It would be a terrible thing to have hiccoughs in the Kremlin. But you couldn't – could you? – be arrested for that.

The car stopped outside the Armoury, that long and severe building which Waring had seen only yesterday from the other side of the wall. To the right he could make out the red flag, flying from the bronze cupola of the Old Senate, the headquarters of the Soviet government. He was in the holy of holies, the forbidden ground. Did he walk, or was he escorted or gently pushed through the great east door of the Arsenal, between the long files of ancient cannon, half seen under the heaped up snow?

He had expected it to be light inside, but it was almost dark. The young soldiers on guard stood rigid to attention as they came in. In the shadows of the great hall, floored with marble checks of black and white, where the ammunition had been piled against the October Revolution, a group of men were standing. Some were Red Army officers in uniform, some were not, and with them was a small man in a dark overcoat. Professor Untermensch had reappeared. Could he be under arrest? If so, why was he smiling and even, apparently, excited?

A command was given which Waring could not hear. The doors opposite flew open, the room beyond sprang into dazzling illumination, and all that Waring could see was gold – not locked away, not in a glass case, but carelessly heaped on floor and tables – the Golden Twine, the Golden Snake and Bird, the Mask and Milk Bowl, the Golden Doll, and, half out of its coffin, the Golden Child itself – unmistakeably authentic, gleaming and darkening, the Golden Treasure of Garamantia.

4

Waring supposed that there was nothing he could complain about.

It was Tuesday morning, and he was on the return flight to London. After his incomprehensible glimpse of the treasure, he had been taken back the four hundred yards to the Hotel Zolotoy by car; his escort, with broad grins, like friendly bruins, had taken him up to his magnificent room, and, too tired to eat, he had passed a sleepless night in the Royal bed, a Romanov still, but a Romanov expecting to face liquidation next morning. The relief when his passport was handed back with the others by the Intourist guide was almost more than he could bear, but even after that, even when the aircraft took off and he was safely and steadily mounting above Moscow airport, he still had to face the now unconcealed hostility of the Suntreaders. Probably they would have liked to wrench his distinguishing travel-labels away from him. They had found out about the bedroom, and had had several hours to discuss his cata-strophic appearance at the House of Friendship. No one would sit next to him, and he heard the phrase 'disgraceful exhibition'. The phrase struck him like a leaden bullet. Leaving his own affairs aside, it reminded him of the Exhibition he was going back to.

What he had seen at the Kremlevskye Arsenal was the real, the genuine treasure. Once seen, it could not be doubted, and the doll in his suitcase, the doll which had not been shown to Semyonov, which served only to frighten a little girl with pigtails, had become for Waring an object of hatred. And the vast, patient public (it would be Schools

93

Day again tomorrow) who would soon be filing across the Museum courtyard to proffer their money at the entrance, what were they paying to see, what imposture was being put before them? And then Waring realised, with the dead certainty of a man who admits at last that the foundations of his house are rotten, that he had known the truth now for almost a week. His body knew it, even if his mind had refused to face it. He still had a sore neck. But how could he have been half choked to death with a piece of twine two thousand years old? It would have crumbled to dust at a touch. What he had felt round his throat, what had been put back into the case, was a ball, quite a new ball, of golden string.

'Someone has to help me,' Waring thought. 'Someone has to explain. I expect not to understand very much, but not not to understand as much as this.'

'This seat is not taken?' said Professor Untermensch, appearing down the gangway, slightly bowing, just as he had at the *stolovaya*.

'You bloody know it isn't,' said Waring. 'What have you done with the rest of the vodka?'

'Oh, it was all exhausted,' said Untermensch, occupying very little space as he sat down. 'And besides, I am not convinced that it was good for you.'

'I expect you're right,' said Waring, sinking his head in his hands. 'Just sit there, will you, and tell me what I'm doing. Not what *you're* doing – I've given up that. Just what I'm doing.'

'There is nothing mysterious about it. You have come here, as you were saying to me, as a very ordinary museum official. Don't be offended! To be ordinary, in these times, is an occasion for bravo! But the Russians do not accept for one moment that that is what you are. They assume you are in the secret service, and that your position in that service is an important one.'

'But what on earth do they think I'm doing?'

'The Soviet Union did not acquiesce in the despatch to

94

London of the Garamantian gold. I realised that as soon as I was shown the toy, and found that it was a replica. The Russians have made a very considerable loan to Garamantia, who is anxious to develop her agriculture; they have lent capital, plant, and technicians and the Russians never grant loans without security. They have therefore, in the manner of a *rostovchik* – a pawnbroker – taken the gold into their keeping for a while. Doubtless they will send it back one day, when Garamantia has found some other means to pay her debt. To avoid fuss, or you may call it an international incident, they must have advised, probably through their East Berlin publicity agency Proklamatius, that the Garamantians should have a passable replica made. Indeed, there may be several replicas.'

'But in that case, if I'm supposed to be a British agent, why did they show it to me?'

'Once again, you forget that the reputation of the British abroad is not one of simplicity, but of cunning. The Russians would not dream that the authorities in London, and the Director of your great Museum, could be taken in by a replica. They think that you have been sent over, with one of the artefacts, simply *to show them that you know*. That is the way their own minds work. They displayed the real treasure to you at the Arsenal, *to show you that they know you know*, and, what pleases them most, that they know that you can do nothing about it. The Exhibition has now been on in London for many days, the populace has been admitted, the children have been instructed, nothing can be done.'

'Is that why they suddenly gave me the best room in the hotel?'

'Ah, so. I did not know that, but I am not surprised. In all oriental diplomacy there is an element of joke.'

'But what were you doing in the Kremlin? Why did they let you in? And, for pity's sake, why have you been following me about?'

'That too is exceedingly simple. They let me in only for the reason that they had seen me following you. To this end I obtained from a 'bargain basement' in your Oxford Street a conspicuous dark coat. You see I still have it on. I was observed; I admit I was afraid that I might have been overlooked, that is why I made my appearance at the circus; but I was observed, and it was assumed that I was one of those who, in every organisation, spies upon its spies. Therefore I too had to be shown *that they knew that I knew*, and I have at last attained the ambition of a life-time; I have seen the golden treasure of Garamantia.'

'Well, I'm glad that you had a successful trip,' said Waring, discovering that he really meant this. 'As far as I'm concerned, it's been a spectacular failure. What about Semyonov? That's a question that's never been answered. That's what I asked them in the House of Friendship. Friendship! I know his address. I know his telephone number. I've spoken to his sister-in-law. I've had two appointments. I had an important message to give him, and I've never even seen him!'

'You will never see Professor Semyonov,' replied Untermensch.

'But I spoke to someone in his flat, a woman, who said he would be back the next day!'

'This was some kindly woman, who did not wish to disappoint you. In fact, Professor Semyonov does not exist.'

'Is he dead?'

'He never existed. To be frank, he is an invention of the Clown Splitov.'

'Invented by a clown! That's not possible! The Director showed me some of his letters!'

'All written by the Clown Splitov.'

'A clown!'

'But a very distinguished one, and an Honoured Artist of the Soviet Union,' said Untermensch consolingly. 'He is frequently used in delicate matters of diplomacy.'

'I can't believe that Sir John Allison, whom I respect so much, can't tell the difference between a clown writing to him and a learned authority . . .'

'That, I admit, is surprising. But the weakness may lie in the translation.'

Waring considered for a few moments.

'And how did you get taken on as a clown at the Circus anyway, just for one evening's performance like that?'

'It was not hard,' Untermensch replied. 'I was well suited to the work. All the artistes at the Tserk Splitov are agents or spies of some kind or another. Incidentally, in the interests of accuracy, I did not appear as a clown, but as an auguste, who does not speak.'

'*All* of them?' Waring persisted. 'Even the man who looked as if he was being hanged?'

'Ah, that one!' said Untermensch. 'He is an agent of the CIA. In my opinion, he is at risk. If I were he, I would resign my employment in the Tserk Splitov.'

Waring tried another direction. 'But how long is all this going on? It can't be kept up much longer! The Exhibition's supposed to be going to Paris after London, then to the States, then to West Berlin . . .'

'There, I think, it will reach the end of its career. If it is definitely proposed to take it to West Berlin, the Russians will threaten, through diplomatic channels, to mount a rival Exhibition in East Berlin, showing, of course, the real Treasure, and under the auspices of no less an authority than the great Professor Semyonov.'

'And what happens to our lot? Our Golden Child?'

'The whole cargo of false riches will disappear,' said the Professor, 'like the Caravans of old, back into the heart of Africa.'

Waring stared out of the porthole, into the impenetrable clouds.

'Anyway, I'm glad you're on this plane. I was beginning to get lonely. We've been having a bit of trouble at home,' – he didn't know why he was telling the Professor all this – 'and, well, I'm very much looking forward to seeing my wife again.'

'I have not seen my wife since 1935,' said the Professor

gently. 'For how long have you been married?'

'Two years, nine months and three weeks,' said Waring. 'It'll be our anniversary soon. We get in at three p.m. our time, don't we? I shall be able to go straight home from Gatwick to Clapham Junction.'

'I am very much afraid that this will not be possible. I think that the Ministry of Defence will want to speak with you.'

As usual, Professor Untermensch was correct. In fantasies, Waring had sometimes watched himself as a tracking shot in a film, greeted at the airport as an important person. He wouldn't have to hang about, wouldn't have to wait while a capricious moving band delivered his luggage last of anybody's; he would be taken, with a nod of understanding, into a separate lounge. And at Gatwick he *was* taken, with a nod of understanding or misunderstanding, into a separate lounge. Two men, giving him from the first the feeling of being outnumbered, advanced on thick, good shoes and singled him quietly out of the file of weary Suntreaders. It was the last drop in their cup of bitterness. He felt their disapproval, grown into something like hatred, following him through the discreet glass door.

'Is anything the matter?' he asked.

'We should be very grateful if you could answer one or two questions. This is in no way an interrogation, of course. We are simply asking if you would be good enough to help us.'

Waring wondered what would happen if he said he wouldn't.

'I'm afraid I'm not quite sure who you are,' he said politely.

There was a slight hesitation. 'My name is Rivett. You can take it that I represent the Ministry of Defence – a branch of the Ministry of Defence. This is my colleague, Detective-Inspector Daniel Gunn, from the Special Branch, who's just joined us for the evening.'

'Then it's a police matter.'

'Call it an enquiry. He's simply joined us for this evening.'

'Well, I should just like to ring up my wife.'

'Of course. No need to go back to the passenger concourse. We have a telephone here.'

Waring didn't care whether they heard him or not. He dialled his home number like a drowning man.

'Haggie!'

She was back again. He was overcome by an intense relief which excluded every other feeling.

'Haggie! You're home again! Is that you? It's me!'

He wasn't expressing himself well.

'I've just come back from Russia ... If you rang the Museum, they must have told you that ... No, it was quite horrible, everything's horrible without you. I can't wait to see you ... Absolutely at once, only I've got to go with these people ... They, well, I can't really tell you properly about them now ... I don't want to see them at all, it wasn't my idea ... Haggie, Haggie, I love you! I couldn't find the launderette bag. I want to be with you more than anything on earth! Haggie, don't go away! Haggie, please!'

Feeling like the unsuccessful end of a cross-talk act, totally wretched, Waring put down the smart new receiver.

'Well, all right. I've got more time than I thought. What did you want me to tell you?'

'Please don't misunderstand us, Mr Smith. It's a matter of what you want to tell us. But not here in any case. Our headquarters for this sort of conversation are outside London – only about twenty miles. We can look after your luggage. Meanwhile the car's here. If you've no objection.'

No objection, except that it's a useless mystification and a waste of taxpayers' money, thought Waring. The headquarters, they added, were not far from Haywards Heath.

It might have been there, or not far from anywhere else, since Waring, who after his bad night had been fast asleep on the drive down, only awoke to see wet bushes of rhododendrons and to hear gravel crunching under the wheels. He felt crumpled. I wonder if they've got an electric razor in there, he thought. And for that matter, what sort of domestic arrangements do they have anyway in a Ministry of Defence interrogation headquarters not far from Haywards Heath? The figure who stood just inside the lighted porch, waiting for orders, looked indistinguishable from a sergeant in the regular army. Waring had a sudden irrational and despairing feeling, which he sternly controlled, that he was never going to get home again at all.

'It's understood that you've been on a confidential assignment for Sir John Allison,' Rivett was saying. 'We have been in touch with Sir John and he doesn't see any harm in your helping us. I take it that you will be making your report to him?'

'I suppose so.'

'But not till, say, the day after tomorrow. The trouble is – although the public may not always believe it – is that we have to move rather quickly. If I could just recapitulate.'

'If you mean, what have I been doing in Leningrad and Moscow, it wouldn't take me very long to tell you.'

'If you don't mind, I'll present the evidence in my own way. There is a professional way of doing it, you know.'

Waring looked at Detective-Inspector Gunn, who sat, apparently in the depths of embarrassment, without contributing anything to the discussion.

'You won't be in any way upset, I'm sure,' continued Rivett, 'when I tell you that you've been under surveillance during your visit to Moscow. Of course without prejudice.'

'Of course.'

'Just a routine business for our men out there. We were, of course, more than a little surprised that Sir John should ask a subordinate to smuggle a valuable piece of worked gold into the Soviet Union. But letting that pass for the moment, our understanding is as follows. You speak Russian fluently, by the way?'

'Up to the end of Book 3. The course ended there.'

'In Moscow you twice failed to make contact with the object of your visit, Professor Semyonov.'

'An invention of the Clown Splitov.'

'What?'

'Never mind,' said Waring. He had just begun to realise that the Ministry of Defence knew a good deal less than he did.

'You did not remain with the other members of your group, but kept what appeared to be an assignation, in a working-class restaurant, with a man who we think was not a Russian, but who was unknown to our observers. All this time you appear to have kept this piece of gold with you. Then, later in the evening, and more surprisingly still, you were taken to the Kremlin itself. There, of course, we were unable to follow your movements. You stayed about a quarter of an hour.'

'I don't know how long it was,' Waring answered, 'but I think I've got the idea. You imagine that I've been trying, with the help of an agent or two, to trade a solid piece of gold, and possibly some kind of information, with the Russians.'

'Please don't think I've said anything as definite as that.'

'Of course not. This is not an interrogation. Just a few questions.'

'We have known things of this kind to happen before.'

'What am I supposed to have done with the gold?'

'We have known replicas to be made, to be taken out when it is time to leave the country. Quite frankly, we should appreciate it if you would allow us to inspect the object you have with you.'

So that's why you offered to look after my luggage, Waring thought, but you didn't find my dolly.

'I'm afraid I can't agree to that. The Doll is the property of the Garamantian government, loaned to the Museum, and I have no authority to show it.'

'Very good,' said Rivett coldly. 'We cannot insist at the moment. We may have the opportunity later.'

'Meanwhile,' Waring went on, 'I should like to tell you something else. My so-called contact in the *stolovaya*, whom your spies didn't know, was a very distinguished international scholar, Professor Heinrich Untermensch. He is known to Sir John Allison, who personally invited him to London, and who I am sure will be only too pleased to vouch for him.'

'I see,' said Rivett. After a pause, he added, 'There may have been an area of misunderstanding.'

'I don't deal in gold,' said Waring, 'or information either. And I should like to know how quickly you can get me home, from somewhere not far from Haywards Heath.'

'You will be driven home, of course. And perhaps I may remind you once again that everything we have said this evening is entirely confidential. I imagine you want to be regarded as someone whose discretion can be relied on; I mean that if it could not, that might affect your promotion, and even your chances of future employment.'

'Really, Mr Rivett,' said Waring, 'if it wasn't for the presence of a police inspector, I should almost believe that I was being subjected to blackmail.'

Rivett looked as though he had not much more to contribute.

'There are one or two further points . . .'

'I don't feel like making any more answers,' said Waring. 'There's someone I want to consult.'

'I thought we had made it clear that this was not a matter for solicitors.'

'I haven't got a solicitor. I can't afford one. That's not what I meant. I want to consult Sir William Simpkin.'

An odd silence fell, and then Inspector Gunn spoke for the first time.

'I'm afraid, sir, that won't be possible. Sir William is dead.'

Sir William had died in the Museum on Friday evening. His body had been found the next morning in the Staff Library, by the daily cleaners. They had instantly summoned Jones.

Poor Jones' immediate reaction had been that it was impossible. Sir William never went down to the library, hated the library because he wasn't allowed to smoke down there, was not too steady on his pins on the stairs, and if he wanted a book Jones fetched it for him, had done just last Tuesday, and it was still on his desk. Yet there the old man was, trapped between two of the sliding steel shelf units, propped upright against the end of a row in the Garamantian section, with one empty old hand hanging pathetically down. His cold pipe was stuffed into his tobacco pocket; curiously enough it had broken into two pieces. No doctor was needed to tell that he was dead.

The object of the steel shelving was to make it possible to house more books. The cases could be pushed together – though this took a considerable effort – like a pack of cards, leaving only one gangway open at a time. Excellent for storage – the system allowed for a forty per cent increase in the stack – it was inconvenient and even alarming for casual readers. The steel shelving by itself could not have killed Sir William. It ran between an upper and lower track and was counter weighted, so that it checked when it met an obstacle.

But if someone had tried to push the shelves together while Sir William was between them, it would have given him a shock, quite enough to precipitate the heart attack which everybody, including himself, expected to kill him sooner or later.

The Director himself saw Jones, and advised him to take as many days' sick leave as he needed. Jones, however, refused to go home. Nor did he resume his ordinary duties, whatever these were, in Stores. He spent the rest of the day, a disturbed and disturbing figure, prowling about the corridors and passages near the library, apparently looking for something.

There were grave and immediate decisions for Sir John to make. First, was he, as a mark of respect, to close the Museum for the day? This was decided against. Sir William's body had not been discovered until half past eight in the morning, and the hordes of visitors were already alighting at the main railway terminals, while Golden Child day trip coaches were making their way through the outer suburbs. Secondly, the media; it now seemed a hopeless matter to prevent the press from running articles, as they had always wanted to do, on the Curse of the Golden Child. Because of Sir John's great personal influence, *The Times* and the BBC still made reference to the 'Curse' or 'the so-called Curse' (the announcers using a special intonation), but both on ITV and in the less expensive papers it became the Horror, the Doom, and the Nameless Dread, while the staff of the Museum were represented as being in a state of pitiable terror. All this Sir John was obliged to leave to his flustered Public Relations staff. Far more urgent and unfortunate were the actual circumstances of Sir William's death, about which only a guarded announcement had been made. The Press Release said that he had died from myocarditis, and so he had. The doctors had no hesitation in giving a certificate, but they pointed out what indeed was obvious enough, that Sir William could not have pushed the shelving units together himself while he was standing between them. Someone else must have done it, and even if they had not seen the old man in the first place, they could not have failed to notice the obstruction when the units jammed and failed to meet. Someone must have known, and they must have walked out of the library and left him there to die.

Sir William, who in his day had scoured the deserts and perilous ruins of the world, had ended as a body in the Library. He was good for years yet, the doctor, a personal friend, said sourly, if it hadn't been for all this nonsense. By 'this nonsense' he meant the Exhibition. The details would have to be sent to the police and to the district coroner.

Nothing could be settled before the inquest, and in this awkward position the Director – who could perhaps be criticised for deciding so many matters single-handed – invited the police to begin their investigations at once. Maintenance and Accommodation were asked to provide a suitable incident room. It must be presumed that they did their best. On the Friday afternoon Detective-Inspector Mace, the crimes officer from King's Cross station, accompanied by Detective-Sergeant Liddell, arrived with their equipment. They were installed in a half-dismantled room which had formerly contained a reserve supply of Aztec musical instruments made with human skin. Most of them had been moved to Ethnographica, but a pile of unpleasant-looking drums remained, together with a cupboard containing a store of sugar and lavatory paper which had been laid in by Maintenance during the shortages, and totally forgotten later.

'No good complaining,' said Sergeant Liddell, looking at the drums. 'I used to collect flints myself when I was a boy.' He opened the cupboard. 'Two lumps, sir, or three?'

The sergeant had done his stretch in the Army before joining the Force and was rapidly able to make them comfortable.

Sir John had asked to let them get on as fast as possible with the preliminary enquiries. He knew what possibilities were threatening him – the Regional Crime Squad, Foreign Office security men with a watching brief, a special investigatory committee on The Curse of the Golden Child, even the Society for Psychical Research. While the general public still poured in through the front entrances and the Press besieged his flank, meddlesome experts and Scotland Yard men would be infiltrating from the back. If only something definite, however unwelcome, could be established immediately, the situation might be kept in control. Sir John offered the two policemen all facilities – except a toilet that works and a gas-pipe that isn't on the point of explosion, said the sergeant later, but Sir John wouldn't know about things like that – and asked them to begin their investigation at once. All difficulties were to be referred back to him personally, and all staff had been instructed to hold themselves ready, if necessary, for interview.

In conclusion the Director regretted that he could be of so little personal assistance. He could confirm that Sir William had been in excellent spirits in the morning, laughing and joking, when he had stepped in for a few minutes to see him. Miss Rank, appealed to, said that the laughter could be heard from one end of the corridor to the other. In the evening Sir John, although he had little time for such functions at the moment, had been obliged to attend a dinner of the Saints and Sinners at the Café Royal; on the way home he had called in to the Museum to pick up some papers which he wished to study for the following day; with a slight feeling of anxiety which he could not now account for, he had sent a messenger up to Sir William's room, but was told that it was empty, although the lights were still on. He assumed that the old man had been sensible enough to go home to bed.

'Did he usually forget to turn the lights out, sir, when he went home?'

'I should have thought not. He was careful in his personal habits and he had been poor when he was young. But on these matters of detail I am afraid you will have to consult my staff.'

The Staff Library was sealed off, and, after taking a number of preliminary statements, the police began work down there. It contained many old volumes, and they were greeted by a strong charnel breath of leather and mould. The library was an eminently plain room, about forty-foot long, the shelving itself forming bays, in each of which was an ancient leather chair. Notices forbidding smoking, and the removal of books, were hung in every bay, and the press marks of the books themselves were related to a mysterious system peculiar to the Museum, which made it difficult and sometimes impossible to find any given title. A grid in the ceiling turned out to be an old-fashioned fire-extinguishing system which, at the pressing of a button, would spray water over the contents of the room, thereby ruining a large number of the books. This, although it had never been used, was in working order and connected to the plumbing of the basement passages, which resembled that of a mighty dreadnought. Along one side of the room, as the result of an unexplained burst of Government generosity, the new steel shelving units had been installed. They glittered incongruously in the half-light of the green-shaded reading lamps.

Inspector Mace tried them out. They moved with a ponderous rattle, but at a touch. The metal surfaces would have to be tested for fingerprints, though without much hope of a definite result; there were hundreds. Sergeant Liddell went obligingly into the Garamantology section and the Inspector several times experimented in trapping him by moving the shelf units. The Sergeant thought the pressure was not much, nothing really, but then he was expecting it, and was a robust man of thirty. The whole library, the catalogues, the files, the stack and the waste-paper baskets revealed nothing dropped or left behind, nothing of interest.

'What beats me is why he should come down here at all,' said the Inspector. 'He could get books brought up to him if he wanted. We've got evidence as to that from the attendant, Jones – not too co-operative, by the way, I thought.'

'He was a bit cut up over Sir William's death.'

'The old-fashioned sort.'

Sergeant Liddell asked what was through the door at the other end, up a short flight of steps. This proved to be the Director's private library, where particularly rare titles, monographs on Renaissance subjects, and a few confidential staff records were kept. It was a most satisfactory room; like everything to do with the Director, quietly unsurpassable. The original leather linings of the shelves were still in place, but so too were a nice little xerox duplicator, an infra-red inspection light, a microcard reader, a collating machine, and safety devices of a much more up-to-date type than those in the main library – quite new, in fact; they discharged carbon dioxide or carbon dioxide snow automatically if the temperature rose above a certain point. They were the first thing that Inspector Mace had really approved of in the Museum. But what particularly caught his attention was a piercingly cold draught. The perfect room was, after all, imperfect. Raised, as it was, slightly above the basement level of the Staff Library, it had a small window opening on to the well of a small courtyard. The draught came from this window. In the centre of the pane a neat square of glass was missing. The edges were broken, but not jagged. There was no sign of any broken glass, either inside or outside the room.

'Anything missing?' asked Sergeant Liddell.

They would have to check that. But a break-in seemed impossible. Only the Director and Miss Rank had keys to the communicating door into the Library, and the access door which opened on to a passage, with the Director's private lift immediately opposite. Miss Rank herself had to admit the cleaner. When the police took her down to see the damage, and to establish that nothing was missing, she permitted herself some signs of emotion.

'The only way to check this kind of thing is a strong hand,' she said. 'It makes you understand why people elect dictators.'

'Do you think there's anyone in the Museum who has a personal grudge against your boss?' the Inspector asked. 'I suppose if the wind and rain had blown this way, some of these books might have been damaged quite badly.'

But he had struck the wrong note with Miss Rank, to whom all forms of gossip were unknown.

'A woman without weaknesses,' he sighed, as she indignantly left the Director's violated sanctum.

'They don't come like that,' said the Sergeant consolingly. 'Give us time, and we'd find one.'

Their investigation was proceeding under very real

difficulties. Apart from the fact that it was only semi-official, since the inquest would not take place till next week, the Inspector struck what he thought of as 'a number of snags'. To begin with, the Director was strongly opposed to the idea of finger-printing his staff. He himself and Miss Rank, as he smilingly pointed out, had already had their prints taken not long ago to set an example to others, when a major theft had been reported in the Museum.

'Yes, I recall that, sir. One of your Egyptian sphinxes removed, wasn't it, just before closing time?'

'The work of an old-age pensioner, I think sir,' put in the sergeant.

The present emergency, the sad death of Sir William, was, the Director pointed out, a totally different matter. To take the prints of Keepers and Executives would seem to suggest an element of criminality in the higher ranks of the Museum.

This was exactly what Inspector Mace *was* suggesting, but he didn't like to say so. 'I've made a bit of a check already at the CRO,' he said. 'It has to be done, of course, sooner or later. There's just one or two points of interest . . . in the catering, for instance – your kitchen superintendent is generally regarded as having a working connection with the Mafia – I thought I'd have a word about him with your Deputy Security; he used to be with us, you know – and then this man I see you've put in charge of the new Jewellery department. Well, he's done a couple of prison sentences.'

'This is very discouraging information,' said the Director.

'Oh, not really, sir, when you consider the number of employees. No one can avoid a few misfits. Then there's this man Leonard Coker. He made a complete statement to us, you know, last week, in connection with the cannabis-growing incident.'

'Coker is not here at the moment.'

'Has he been fired?'

'It was thought that he ought to take some days of unpaid leave to consider his position.'

So that's what they call it here, thought the Inspector. 'Well, perhaps I could see Coker at his home address,' he said, 'and we'll defer the matter of finger-printing for the moment.'

Even more frustrating, and much more unintelligible, was a certain directive, not addressed directly to the Inspector but to someone very much higher up in the Police Force, which was felt to have a strong but obscure bearing on the whole investigation. It was a suggestion, or perhaps something even less definite than that, from the Foreign Office that any enquiries which seemed to lead to indications tending in a certain direction should be, very discreetly, dropped. Inspector Mace, after an early morning session with his District Commander, had emerged – for he was a shrewd man – with only one perfectly clear idea. Whatever happened, he wasn't very likely to get his promotion this time round.

Then there were the irritating small points: for example, the bright yellow leaflets – GOLD IS FILTH, FILTH IS BLOOD – leaflets which, the police were given to understand, had been mysteriously distributed in the courtyard on the first Public Day. It hadn't taken long to establish that they had been printed on the Museum's private press – not much in demand nowadays, most of the work was sent out. Someone must have wanted, at this early stage, to discredit or perhaps even to close the Exhibition. But exactly who had given the order to print these particular leaflets was, so far, unclear.

At least there was no objection to an examination of Sir William's room. Perhaps Sir William's secretary might prove a bit more approachable than Miss Rank. But Miss D. Vartarian, it turned out, was in hospital.

'You might take that as your job, Liddell. Give them a ring at the Bedford Hospital and ask if you can go and chat her up in the ward. Just an informal statement. She may know why anyone would want to leave an old man to die like that.'

'I don't know why anyone would. We don't know about

the money yet, though,' said the Sergeant. He was brewing up in the depressing incident room.

'No, we don't,' replied the Inspector, 'except the bequest to Sir John and that would have come to him soon enough, anyway. That was to be used for the Museum, of course.'

'But there may have been personal bequests that someone couldn't wait for. Or someone might have been jealous of Sir William.'

'Jealous of what, sir? It beats me what they do all day. I mean, look at it any way you want, it doesn't add up to a day's work. A bit of crowd control, but Security look after that. I mean, the things are all in their cases, nothing to do there. I suppose they've got to see the labels are the right way up.'

'We're not here to pass judgment on them, we're here to help them out of a hole,' rejoined Inspector Mace. 'Still, I can see what you're getting at. But they're always re-arranging things nowadays, you know, and that makes work.'

'I expect when this Exhibition closes they'll feel an ugly gap. They'll have to look round for things to do then.'

'Like cleaning out this cupboard,' said Sergeant Liddell. 'They could start on that.'

Both felt exhilarated by the idea of undertaking something as definite as an examination of Sir William's desk. They started with high hopes, but it was soon evident that the old man had nothing to be ashamed of, nothing to hide. There were letters from his long-dead wife, and a lock of hair in an envelope; there was nowhere else for him to keep them, except the club. There were faded photographs of expeditions in distant summers, and a treasured postcard of Sinai from Sir Flinders Petrie himself. A notebook in a locked drawer contained a list of charitable donations which Sir William had made anonymously, and notes on hard luck cases which had come to his notice. Another drawer was entirely full of pipes; there were some which had been sent as presents from all over the world; one correspondent from

Papua sent a new clay pipe every year, and could not know as yet that no more would be needed. There were drafts for memoranda which Sir William had made, and never finished, on alternative schemes for public viewing, on avoiding the extreme frustration and boredom of the queues, and on the very doubtful legality of charging extra for special exhibitions. In the right-hand top drawer, quite openly on display among postage-stamps, fishing-hooks and string, was a copy of Sir William's last will and testament, made and dated three years earlier.

Inspector Liddell read the will cautiously; he already knew that Sir William had sometimes whiled away the tedium of old age with little jokes; it seemed pretty certain, however, that this was simply a duplicate of a valid legal document. The gift to Sir John was mentioned, as explaining why there were no further gifts to the Museum which had been the testator's home for so long. Then came pages of scrupulous donations to charities and foundations, to club servants, to distant relatives and to individuals whom he had liked, or been sorry for. Among these were Jones, who was to receive £2,000 in token of his loyal services; Mr Waring Smith, £8,634.65p, 'because this is the amount necessary to clear him with the Whitstable and Protective Building Society'; Miss Dousha Vartarian, £5,000 'because raising a family is, to all appearances, an expensive business'. A codicil directed the sale of a partnership in a gold mine which Sir William had only just recalled, in order to finance 1) an annual scholarship for a young London boy wishing to study field archaeology, 2) an extension doubling the width of the Museum's famous portico, so that there would be twice as much covered accommodation for students wishing to eat their sandwiches. Nothing was to be named after him, no memorial was specified, he had no living relations. He was content to disappear quietly out of life, having earned every penny he had, and having, after all, had pretty good value in giving it away as he liked.

Sir William's solicitors confirmed that, 'to the best of their knowledge' – for like all solicitors they appeared to keep their knowledge in various qualities – the document was accurate and in fact a draft of the will at present in their possession.

'Right,' the Inspector said. He had a feeling of getting somewhere. 'We have to interview the people who could reasonably be supposed to have access to the Library – not bad, there's not so many of them – and out of those the ones that were working late here on Friday night. The doctor's established the time of death as between 7 and 10 p.m., so that's our limits more or less laid down. Then, out of that lot again, we might as well start with those that had a motive for getting rid of Sir William, that's to say, the beneficiaries under this will. Out of the list, W. Smith is apparently abroad, expected back on Tuesday, definitely wasn't here Friday; Jones had a key although he hadn't any right to it; D. Vartarian we know is hospitalised. Liddell, see if you can contact this Jones.'

A request was sent out, but Jones was not in Stores, and although he had been seen 'hanging about in the little courtyard outside the library' earlier in the day, he could not be found at the moment. Jones, in fact, was rarely found unless he wanted to be.

'There was another one, quite high up, a Keeper, staying late in that part of the building on Friday. He's down as M. Hawthorne-Mannering. He wasn't working, he appears to have been giving a dinner-party.'

'Rather him than me,' said the Sergeant. 'I can't say I feel a festive atmosphere in this place.'

'There's an executive dining-room upstairs, with white tablecloths and so on. He was entertaining a visiting nut called Rochegrosse-Bergson, if I've got the name right. In my opinion we'd better talk to them both.'

'Hawthorne-Mannering. Well, sir, it was his office rang through earlier to ask if we could see him as soon as possible because he's anxious to leave for the weekend. It seems he has a place in the country.'

The Keeper of Funerary Art glided in and, looking exceptionally out of place on one of the coarse and creaky chairs provided in the incident room, confirmed the matter of the dinner-party. It had been entirely private, arranged by himself.

'Yes, certainly, a little celebration *à deux* . . . or one might say, an *amende honorable* . . . and of course, a new friendship . . .'

'Did you or your guest at any time during the evening go down to the Staff Library?'

'Oh, we did, we did. We directed ourselves downstairs . . .'

'This "directed ourselves", sir, if you'll excuse me – does that suggest that you may have had a certain amount to drink?'

'A direct translation from the French . . . but certainly one took wine . . . the atmosphere was exciting, not to say vibrant.'

'Very well, sir, we'll leave it at that. Did you and your guest need to consult any book in particular?'

'No *need* – it was a passing fantasy. One has become – although it is quite outside one's field – fascinated with Garamantology. We were both taken by a whim to write to a mutual friend, a dear friend, now living in Tangiers, and it seemed to us both that it would be amusing to write in the Garamantian hieroglyphics – of course, quite unknown to us both – but we thought we would consult a book on the subject to see if certain practices, certain attitudes, call them that, could be expressed in picture writing.'

Hawthorne-Mannering smiled faintly in reminiscence. This one's certainly at his ease, thought the Inspector.

'Did you find what you were looking for?' he asked.

'No, no, the volume was unfortunately out – the first volume of Heinrich Untermensch's *Garamantischengeheimschriftendechiffrierkunst.*'

Sergeant Liddell paused in his shorthand note. Blanks for some of these proper names, he decided.

'Now, sir, could you tell me whether, while you were in the Library, you noticed whether anyone else was there at all?'

'No one.'

'No one came in or left?'

'No one.'

'And the lights were not on when you entered the library?'

'No, total darkness.'

'Did you alter the position of the steel shelving?'

'I think the shelves were open at the right section. The steel is so cold to the touch. Personally, I was against the installation.'

'Quite, sir. Now, exactly what time would this be?'

Hawthorne-Mannering smiled again. He had absolutely no idea.

'Then perhaps you could tell me what time it was when you returned home?'

'One took a taxi . . .'

'If any recollection as to the time should come to you, we should be very grateful if you'd inform us. Meanwhile, if I might trouble you on one more point: this Mr – no Dr – Rochegrosse-Bergson: did he know Sir William Simpkin well?'

'Very slightly, I should say.'

'It has been suggested to me that he was somewhat disconcerted at this conference, or meeting, when Sir William suggested that he was going under an assumed name.'

Hawthorne-Mannering grew visibly stiffer, as though crystallising. 'Who told you that?'

'Sir John Allison mentioned it to me.'

'I have no idea what he could mean.'

'Well, sir, not to worry. I shall be seeing Dr Bergson myself tomorrow and we can doubtless clear it up then.'

The Inspector was waiting, in fact, for a call from an acquaintance of his at the Sûreté before going any further. Hawthorne-Mannering was disturbed.

'I rely on you to see that this very distinguished visitor is in no way harassed or insulted. He will soon be returning to Paris after a round of scholarly discussions, and one must ensure that his impressions . . .'

'Don't worry, sir, you can leave all that sort of thing to us. But perhaps, just in conclusion, you wouldn't mind telling me, were you yourself in Sir William's confidence?'

'In no sense. Sir William's ideas were not one's ideas, and his ways were emphatically not one's ways.'

'You did not see eye to eye with Sir William?'

'I hated him.'

The policemen both had a shrewd idea that this distinguished visiting scholar might receive a hint that it would be wiser to depart. Mace was relieved when his call from Paris came through with exceptional promptness. Then, leaving by a back exit to avoid the overwhelming Saturday afternoon queue, he and his sergeant took a taxi to a hotel in South Kensington.

'What did you think of that Hawthorne-Mannering?' the Inspector asked.

'Well, he seemed an educated man.'

'He was frank enough about hating Sir William.'

They skirted the Park and drew up at a glittering block.

Both of them were impressed, when they were admitted to the suite reserved by Rochegrosse-Bergson, to find him seated at a table, the subdued light gleaming from his silver hair and shoe-buckles, apparently in the middle of writing a book. This in spite of the fact that he could not possibly have known that they were coming. Perhaps he was always ready for visitors. Pages lay under his hand in picturesque confusion.

'We're sorry to interrupt, sir, if you're just in the middle of composing something.'

'Do not apologise, Inspector. In this situation, if we are to refer back to our archetypes, I am the sage, you are the *numbskull*. In the folk-tales, the apologues, the intervention of the numbskull is often of great value. You will recall the tale of the man who sewed up the neck of his shirt and asked his wife to cut off his head, so that he could put his shirt on?'

'I can't see why that was of great value,' said the Inspector.

'I am illustrating merely. I am simply suggesting that you, M. L'Inspecteur, without knowledge of art, may yet solve the little secrets of the Museum.'

Inspector Mace, who had trained with the Art Squad, and collaborated on the International Art Register, received this without comment.

'What little mysteries might you be referring to, sir?'

'Ah, you must tell me that, Inspector, that's your *métier*.'

'There's no mystery about what we're doing, sir, none at all. We're simply enquiring into the circumstances of the death of Sir William Simpkin.'

'His accidental death, yes.'

'Were you a close friend of Sir William's?'

'Hardly at all, I regret . . .'

'But you gave your conference last Wednesday in his room?'

'That was a courtesy merely.'

'Now, on this occasion I am informed that Sir William made some reference to your change of name?'

'I am surprised that you have heard this; the conference was entirely private.'

'Your name was in fact formerly Schwarz?'

'If it amuses you to think so.'

'You changed your name to Rochegrosse-Bergson after a State Prosecution in 1947?'

'If I was in prison in 1947, it is likely that I was in good company.'

'And may I ask, sir, what was your occupation during the war itself?'

'All that a poor infirm could do. I guarded my little provincial Museum at Poubelle-sur-Loire. You know it, perhaps, Inspector? Beautifully housed in an old Hôtel de

Dieu, although not much visited by the good citizens of Poubelle.'

'Numbskulls, I daresay,' put in Sergeant Liddell.

Rochegrosse-Bergson stared at him. 'Your subordinate?'

'I don't know the museum at Poubelle,' continued the Inspector firmly, 'but I do know that it had very respectable holdings – a collection of baroque pearl jewellery, a Fouquet, a Nattier, and a Rembrandt – *Two Women Sewing by Lamplight.*'

'That is so, yes. A small Rembrandt.'

'None of these things are in the museum now?'

'Some losses have been acknowledged.'

'Including the Rembrandt?'

'Yes.'

'It has never been recovered?'

'Not to my knowledge.'

'There was no insurance?'

'A little provincial gallery! We could never have paid the premiums.'

'A little gallery which has found itself forced to close,' the Inspector said. 'Now, I think I am right in saying that in France there is a law of limitations – an owner can no longer reclaim his stolen property after thirty years have passed. That time, I suppose, will just about have expired.'

'It appears so. You have made the calculation for me.'

'Now, sir, when Sir William made that allusion to your name, indicating I suppose that he knew your past history quite well, did you feel that this was a potentially awkward or dangerous situation for you?'

'It was said in private.'

'But among people on whom I suppose you hoped to make a good impression?'

'I am not concerned with the impression I make. My conference was valued at its true worth.'

'But in spite of that, and in spite of the little dinner which I understand was given for you, did you perhaps feel that Sir William might be better out of the way?'

With a pantomime of unconcern, Rochegrosse-Bergson let his fingers play over his typewriter. 'I decline to answer further questions. The time I have given you already is time stolen from literature.'

'Will you let him go?' asked Sergeant Liddell.

'Yes, back to Paris. Then check again with the Sûreté.'

'What happened to all those things in his museum?'

'He's said to have sold them to various industrialists, one by one. He gave out that the Germans had taken them during the Occupation.'

'Do you reckon Sir William knew that?'

'He seems to have known a good deal.'

'Well, sir, what next? We've been on since 7.46 and it's now 16.42, just in case you'd like a time check, sir.'

'I know it, Sergeant. But I still want to interview Jones. Surely they must have unearthed him by now. A word with Jones and I'd call it a fair day's work.'

Sergeant Liddell resigned himself. They had to use the back door of the Museum as before, and even there it was difficult to find any of the warding staff in the thronging crowds. One of the door attendants ran past them, almost knocking them down; the police recognised the beginnings of panic.

'Tell Jones I want to talk to him,' said the Inspector, standing firm as a rock.

'He can't talk to you. He can't talk to anyone. He fell out of a window on the fifth floor ten minutes ago. He's smashed to pieces.'

5

When Waring Smith reached home he felt so battered, so much more knowledgeable and so much less confident that he scarcely knew what he was supposed to do next. His good sense told him that he had better go back to work at the usual time next morning, and make as acceptable a report as he could on his expedition.

As soon as he picked up the newspapers, lying in reproachful disorder on the front door-mat, he learned the details of Sir William's death. Then, in the Sundays, came a long paragraph on the death of Jones. In stunned disbelief, Waring could only remember Sir William asking why the blazes the public shouldn't believe there was a Curse on the Treasure if they wanted to.

He rose early to go to the launderette before starting out to work; there, sitting between a sleeping tramp and a West Indian mother of six, with his shirt and socks whirling round before his eyes, he allowed himself to think, or to feel, rather. All the springs of emotion, frozen up in him, first by the exactions of the Whitstable and Protective Building Society, then by the bewilderment of his Russian trip, were now set free. Even the enormity of the truth about the Exhibition receded, and he was totally absorbed by his longing for Haggie and his grief for the loss of Sir William. Yes, Sir William had been eighty-five, and his life depended on a hairsbreadth from day to day. But he had filled a place which now had to stand forever empty. How kind, and how unkind he had been at exactly the right moments, and how impressive, distinct and apart, with the patina of fine old age on him, like the Museum's choicest objects, detached and yet affectionate towards the queer century into which he had survived. He had cared about the patient public outside the Museum, not out of sentimentality, not even because he had been born in the backroom of a two-up-two-down in Poplar, but as a plain matter of justice. He could not imagine the Museum without the chance of going up to Sir William's room, dense with smoke from morning till evening, for a few words about heaven knows what.

The papers also spoke about an inquest, and that was a hard blow. Waring would very much have liked the old man to have been buried in peace. In any case, it was all nonsense. How could Sir William have collapsed and died in the Library? He never went there.

Even in the few days he had been away, the aspect of the queues had changed. The courtyard, an hour before admission time, had more the appearance of a great fair painted by Breughel; the weather was almost as cold as in Moscow, tiny children in bright woollen hats were chasing each other in and out of the legs of the crowd, and enterprising vendors of hot dogs and meat pies had been allowed to set up their pitch under the colonnades. As Waring came into work, showing his Museum pass, the police were moving away a one-man band.

'Gently, officer, I was only keeping their spirits up with song and dance,' the shabby musician complained. Queueing to see the Golden Child, whether accursed or not, had evidently become an accepted way of life, and Waring had the impression that the crowd had pitched their tents in the wind-swept desert before the Museum for ever.

The warding staff were glad to have a new audience for their gloomy speculations. They, very naturally, were much more concerned with the death of Jones than with that of Sir William. Jones, with his anomalous position, had been the subject of much disapproval during his lifetime; it was not so now. Waring was told that Jones was a kind of martyr, having, if you could put it like that, given his life for Sir

William, whatever way you took it. Either he did himself in out of grief – no one for a moment entertained the idea of an accident – or he was pushed, for it was known beyond controversy that he had discovered something, somehow or other, about Sir William's death and was on his way to tell the Director about it. He had dropped a hint about this. He had not gone up by the lift, but by the stairs. Why hadn't Jones gone to the police? Well, he was the sort of lonely bugger, if you get my meaning, who had to be devoted to someone; when Sir William was gone, he seemed to kind of turn towards the Director.

'It's a pity you weren't here for the funeral yesterday, Mr Smith – Jones' funeral. It was at Willesden. Not many came. It seemed like as though he hadn't any relatives at all. We all subscribed for a wreath, of course. It didn't really bear thinking of. They had to recover what they could of him from No. 3 forecourt outside the Assyrian rooms.'

'I wish I'd been able to come to the funeral,' said Waring. 'Sir William would have liked to have been there too.'

'I take your meaning, Mr Smith.'

'And what are they going to do about Sir William?'

'There's going to be a memorial service at St Paul's. Admission by ticket, but we don't know how they're going to allocate the tickets among the various grades. You'll find there's a fair amount of discussion going on about that.'

On his somewhat reluctant way up to work, Waring had to pass the Press Department, who were in a state of turmoil. The sensitive friends of Hawthorne-Mannering, the cultured correspondents of the better papers, my friend Peter Gratsos, and so forth, were at a discount. Reporters and strangers fought their way into the ill-prepared department, refused to accept hastily printed handouts on the subject of the Curse, tripped over the trailing cables of TV and broadcasting companies, and clashed with the serious emissaries of American universities who were trying to conduct field surveys, under strictly controlled conditions, of the visitors to the exhibition, to see which of them, if any, had been blasted or withered by the confrontation with the Golden Child. It was not difficult to find people emerging from the exhibition who felt funny, or felt that they had come over funny while in the Burial Chamber, and their degrees of funniness, Waring saw, were being programmed into an acceptable form so that the Curse could be evaluated by a computer. But the exhibition consisted of forgeries and modern imitations; so what was the force, Waring wondered, of an imitation Curse?

He was passing now by the back entrances of the Exhibition itself, and it occurred to him, as a sudden unexpected illumination, that he would very much like to see again the object which represented his last contact with Sir William – the clay tablet which he had been asked to put back in Case VIII. The conviction, quite unsupported by any reasoning, that he had been given it for a special purpose, and that Sir William hadn't really expected him to put it back without looking at it, grew on him more and more. What a marked thing, what an absurd thing, it had been, when all was said and done, to ask him to come back at that time of night to the Museum, simply to put an uncatalogued clay tablet back where it belonged! The morning would have done well enough. Waring let himself in at one of the back doors, feeling, as he always did, miserably apologetic towards those nearly half a mile back at the end of the queue. He was in the second room. He did not want to look at the rest of the exhibits at the moment; he knew that he was looking at replicas worth not much more than the value of the gold leaf that decorated them, and that all the hard work which he and so many others had put in had been in the service of a gigantic swindle. Think about that later; meanwhile he went straight to Case VIII. He looked carefully, walked all the way round it, and looked again; there was no doubt about it – the tablet was gone.

Had the loss been reported, and, if not, should he report it? The enormity of all the monstrous events which had attended the exhibition since the first peaceable committee meetings, to decide on the available space, weighed upon Waring as though, once again, he had been half suffocated. Better go and do some work, and, though he had not been allowed to do that lately, to mind his own business. Then, as he reached his tiny familiar office, the last on the left in the third corridor on the right, his heart seemed to flounder and stop. His name had disappeared from the door, and when he opened it there was nothing left on his desk. His books and drawing-board were gone, so was his paper-weight, a piece of marble from Iona which Haggie and he had picked up on their honeymoon. They had taken away everything, even his chair; a clean sweep.

It was like a sinister reminiscence of the evening at the Hotel Zolotoy, except that there were two letters in the in-tray, both addressed to himself. Hope came back with the shock of individuality which the sight of one's own name written down always brings. Sitting uncomfortably on the edge of the desk, he opened the first one; it was an Internal Memorandum.

FROM: Keeper of Funerary Art.
TO: Mr W. Smith
There has been some slight reorganisation during your absence and your new appointment, one understands, will be that of P.A. to the Director. It would be best if you had a word with me as soon as possible, simply to clarify the position.

M.H.-M.

The other letter was in a dirty and crumpled envelope, and addressed in a pointed continental hand.

Dear Mr Smith,
    My condolences on what has passed, and on the loss of one who was your friend. I stay now with Mr Leonard Coker, which may perhaps be surprising to you, that he and I may

discuss certain matters. Enquire for me, please, to his apartment over the Café Megaspeilon in Ithaca Street.

Sincerely,

Heinrich Untermensch.

At least, Waring reflected, I needn't feel unwanted. It's better than I thought. The clearance of his room was, at least partly, explained. But the non-possession of a chair and of a fixed whereabouts in the vast building made him a naked man, unbelonging and unplaced. He must find out what was happening, how his salary would be affected, what they had done with his things. Normally, if they were really transferring him, he would have been required to go through the leisurely processes of the Establishment Department. But now, though for what reason he couldn't conceive, all, apparently, that he had to do was to see the May Queen.

Hawthorne-Mannering was in. Though frequently weary, he was always punctual.

'Your job, ah yes, one does know something about that. You will be going up a grade – you will be an AP4. You will no longer be working in direct contact with the exhibition.' A shade of satisfaction crept into his voice. 'You will be working very closely with Sir John Allison, in fact as a junior personal assistant, particularly I think over the next three weeks, while his secretary, Veronica Rank, will be away on her annual holiday. Miss Rank, in fact, is the only person who will be able to explain your duties to you in detail, and you're to report to her early tomorrow morning, at eight-thirty, if you'll make a note of that.'

As an AP4 Waring's salary should start at £3,957. But exactly what would he have to do for it?

'You appear rather bewildered by this sudden promotion.'

But Waring was not. He understood it very well, and was only wondering whether even the extra money was worth it. He had nothing but respect and admiration for Sir John

Allison, but he was not such a fool as to think he could assist him in any way. He supposed he ought to seize the opportunity, shine, recommend himself to the great Director; but the truth was, he was an exhibition planning and lay-out man; he could do that well, and he enjoyed it, but was not at all sure that he would be competent at anything else. Furthermore, he wasn't being promoted on account of any abilities he had, that was transparently clear. He was being kept an eye on, because nobody yet knew what he had seen or found out in Moscow – the Golden Doll was still in his suitcase – and, much more important, whether he might not talk too much, and, in his inexperience, give away unwelcome truths to the wrong people.

He got up. 'Thank you very much. Miss Rank tomorrow, at eight-thirty.'

'Just a moment,' said Hawthorne-Mannering, with apparent casualness, 'How did the little pilgrimage to Moscow work out?'

So he knows about it too, Waring thought. That's why he wanted to see me. 'I think I managed to do what was wanted,' he said.

'And Professor Semyonov?'

Waring hesitated. 'I think he's easier to deal with by letter than by personal interview. But, as perhaps you know, I was told to make my report personally to the Director.'

'Of course, of course. One stands reproved.'

'I didn't mean that.' It struck Waring that Hawthorne-Mannering was looking particularly queer today. Perhaps he ought to say something rather less grudging by way of what was a kind of farewell. Waring knew that he himself had hardened over the last few days. His puppyish desire to please and convince had gone, and had been replaced by a new perception, with which as yet he had not quite come to terms, as to how the world was run.

'I'd like to say how much I've enjoyed working with the Exhibition,' he said. 'I shall be very sorry to leave it. That's what interests me most – the point of contact with the public. I know that there are some people in the service who'd rather not have them let in at all, or restricted to certain days. Of course I was much too junior to have any kind of say in that, but I did feel strongly about it, and still do.'

'It has been much discussed,' replied Hawthorne-Mannering, 'but our relationship with the public is hardly my field – it hardly concerns me. One has kept quite apart from it. One's hands are clean!'

One's hands are clean! He shot his elegant cuffs and spread out his hands in the familiar, half-automatic gesture. Waring stared at them for a second in fascination, and immediately, as though struck by embarrassment and even terror, Hawthorne-Mannering tried to hide them. It was too late. Waring sprang up, and, reaching across the desk, grasped the two willowy wrists. They felt like the air-filled bones of a bird, writhing in his firm hold. Across the two white palms was a thin strong red line, the mark of cord or string.

'It was you that went for me that night! It was you who put the Golden Twine round my neck! It's the mark! I thought it was Len. You filthy-well half-strangled me!'

Hawthorne-Mannering shrank and twisted. 'You are making a very great fool of yourself, Smith. Your head is turned. The Golden Twine! It would crumble to dust . . .'

'Not if it was plain ordinary string. It is, and you knew that. The whole bloody exhibition is a fake, it's a myth, and it seems as if everyone knows it except the tens of thousands out there on the pavement.'

'What does it matter?' whimpered Hawthorne-Mannering. 'They have come to be amazed, and they are amazed. What more can they ask?'

'Why did you do it?' said Waring fiercely, and fiercely resisting a temptation to shake him. 'Funerary art! You murderer, you half-murderer, why did you have to go for me?'

'I hated you! You trespassed. You went out of your field.

127

When I was laid low, you stole my credit – you crapped your petty little descriptions and attributions into my catalogue. What were you doing in the exhibition that night? Spying, taking notes – preparing a monograph which might anticipate mine! I saw the Golden Twine. I was tempted – yes, tempted – the last thing in the world I should have chosen. I did not think of the consequences to myself – I wanted to frighten you. I strongly desired to see you choked lifeless – but one held one's hand!'

'One heard someone coming and ran away,' said Waring. 'God in heaven, do you mean you strangled me on account of a catalogue?'

'You don't understand . . .'

'I understand this. I've been overworked and insulted. I've been run through the foot with a fish-spear. I've been garrotted. I've been packed out of the country. I've been made to look the most almighty bloody idiot in the Union of Soviet Republics. I've been processed by MI5. I've lost my job. I've lost my wife. And yet for some reason I can't account for, the thing that matters to me most is to know what happened to Sir William and how he died. You poor sod, you fish-fingered exquisite, did you have anything to do with it?'

Hawthorne-Mannering had sunk back. His remaining strength appeared to be draining away. There was no use in pressing for the truth there. Waring relaxed his grip on the fragile wrists and let him go.

'What are you going to say about this?' Hawthorne-Mannering asked faintly. 'Will you find it necessary to mention it to anyone? To the press? To the police?'

'No,' said Waring.

'I am obliged. One's career would be affected.'

Now that he was free from Waring's grip, however, Hawthorne-Mannering apparently rallied. He sat almost upright and, keeping his hands carefully turned palms downward, suddenly said in an altered voice, 'You may go, Smith. This had been an untrustifiable injuiceson.'

Waring looked at him in dismay. What's come over the May Queen? he thought. Has it been too much for him? I know I mixed things up a bit in Moscow, after the vodka, but surely I wasn't like this? And anyway, it's only ten o'clock. Hawthorne-Mannering seemed conscious that something was not quite right.

'One is stuffering from sain . . .'

'Perhaps you ought to consult someone?'

'Yes . . . yes . . . under octor's dorders . . .'

'That would probably be for the best,' said Waring. 'I'm only going to tell you one more thing. You can trust me not to bring up this subject again, and I might add that I've no intention of writing a monograph. But you owe me a good turn, remember that. And I shall very likely ask for it.'

Hawthorne-Mannering nodded a feeble assent. I don't think my responsibilities extend to calling a doctor, Waring told himself, but he does look queer, almost transparent. He asked if he could do anything or get anything, and was told, in a faint murmur, to tall a caxi. Hawthorne-Mannering was going to retreat to the sheltering care of Poynton, his family home in Dorset.

When Waring had spoken of good turns, rather more calculatingly than was natural to him, he had been thinking of Len's job. The Warding Staff had told him that Mr Coker had unquestionably been sacked, as the result, they added, of knocking up dangerous drugs in the basement. Waring didn't know how easy Len would find it to get employment under these circumstances, and, in his way, the Keeper of Funerary Art was a man of influence.

Meantime, he couldn't see that he himself would be needed at the Museum until the next morning. He asked whether Sir John Allison would be in that day, but was told that the Director had had to go to Switzerland, in connection with a possible transfer of the exhibition to Geneva; he would not be back till tomorrow afternoon.

Waring's mind went back to the subject of Len. He owed Len an apology for having thought he'd tried to strangle him with a bit of string; that had been all wrong, and he wouldn't feel it was put right until he had told Len about it. There was plenty of time before to call at the address above the Megaspeilon Café; there was all day, in fact, and if, as appeared from his letter, the Professor was also there, that would be all the better. Waring had met by this time quite a lot of scholars, quite a lot of single-minded experts, but none of them, except Untermensch and Sir William himself, had possessed much heart.

By an association of ideas which he didn't bother to make clear to himself, Waring thought he might ring up home just once again, even though he risked, for the dozenth time, the unmistakeable sound, the idiotic repetition of a telephone ringing in an empty flat. He summoned his courage, dialled, and Haggie answered.

She was back, and she agreed to meet him. She observed, gaily and quite accurately, that they had not been out together for a long time. 'Don't bother to come home first,' she said. 'I shall have to have my hair cut. I'm going to have it all off. It'll look different.'

Waring felt he would have preferred her not to do this, but had enough sense not to say so. They could meet, say, at half-past six and have something to eat, or something, and see a film, or something. They could meet at the Dominion in Tottenham Court Road.

Waring felt delirious. It was all over; things were going to be just as they had been before. She had said nothing about her departure to Hackney. He, for his part, had saved up the news that he had become an AP4, and that the Whitstable and Protective, though still formidable, would be less menacing. A little extra money made a lot of difference. A visit to the hairdresser, it was true, often proved disastrous, Haggie regretting the style which had been decided on at the very moment of leaving the shop; but she would get over it, her hair would grow, life would renew itself, his bed would be warm again, they would be happy as sure as grass was green.

He went out through the great revolving doors and looked down the steps at the ever-crowded courtyard. Weightless and free in the unexpected moment of happiness, he was overtaken by a quite unexpected impulse: he felt that he must – it was as strong as that – join the queue and see the Golden Treasure not as a museum official, but as an ordinary payer of 50p admission. Sir William, who had always wanted to do this, but had been too old, had urged Sir John to try it; but Sir John, whose face was very familiar to the public as the result of his lengthy TV series, *What is Culture?*, in which he had appeared in close-up against all the better-known works of art in Western Europe, felt that he was certain to be recognised. Waring, however, was not justifying himself, or acting as an observer, or looking for an experience. He simply went out in his raincoat and, guided by some dim but strong instinct, took his place at the far end of the courtyard, at the very end of the six-times winding column of the queue.

The doormen saw him go, and tapped their foreheads significantly. Mr Smith was going the same way as Jones. Worse would follow. And Mr Hawthorne-Mannering had just left in a cab, looking frightful.

Waring had taken up his stance only for a few moments when others closed in behind him. He was surrounded and accepted, and on both sides people began to talk to him, in the glow of shared endurance. He was told that he was lucky today, there was only three-and-three-quarter hours wait. However did they arrive at such exact figures? The length of time waited was, it soon emerged, an important part of the experience of seeing the Treasure. Some, indeed it seemed to Waring most, of the queuers had seen the Exhibition several times – anything up to twenty. One woman, not at all strong-looking, and accompanied by several children, had seen it every day since it opened. Tomorrow there was the extension time, the extra public opening from six till eight, so she would be coming twice. These people were well-adapted to the conditions, and were dressed, not like the Suntreaders, but rather as in photographs which Waring remembered to have seen of the Blitz. In fact, the clothes *were* largely of that era, having been mostly acquired from government surplus stores. The multitude wore RAF anoraks, Air Raid Wardens' greatcoats, simulated sheepskin flak jackets and postmen's gabardines. They had portable cooking-stoves, short-wave transistor radios to while away the hours, and duckboards to cross the puddles. Heaven knew how the Museum cloakrooms were coping with this load of paramilitary equipment. But, Waring was told, they had had nothing like this in the early pioneering days, a couple of weeks ago. The First Ten Thousand! One or two spoke up, who had actually experienced these rigours. A kind of badge, representing two sore feet on a golden background, had been issued to those who could show that they had queued – there had never been a time without a queue – during the first three days.

Waring was disconcerted to find that nearly everyone appeared to be rather hazy, even perhaps not very interested, about what they had actually come to see. Old hands described the Treasure only vaguely. 'You'll find it's all real gold!' He felt a little reassured when he was told that you couldn't really get up your interest until you got a couple of hundred yards from the building. It made the time go quicker if you didn't think about it till then.

A few snowflakes fell, and the children put out their tongues to taste the freezing crystals. Waring felt transported in space and time to the Alexandrovskaya Park. The true international solidarity was not between workers, but between queuers.

Waring stuck out the three-and-three-quarter hours – nearly four hours in the end – and reached the last stretch at about three o'clock. The telephone call and the companionable wait in the queue had made him completely happy. He no longer felt lonely, and he was free of the obscure weights which had seemed to oppress his spirit. But as the main entrance loomed only fifty yards away, a change came over the queue. It was like the custom, on mediaeval pilgrimages to Santiago de Compostella, when the first pilgrim to see the twin bell-towers of the cathedral flung his staff in the air, and received the name of 'King'. In the same way an informative man, who was just able to hear what was being said at the entrance, received the silent attention of the queue as he relayed the information that regrettably each visitor would only be allowed ten minutes in the Museum, and twenty seconds to pass in front of the Golden Child itself. Everyone began to get out their money, although it would be a considerable time before it was needed. They took one glove off to count the coins, blew on their stiffening fingers, put the glove back. At this point, again entirely on an impulse, Waring slipped away unnoticed. He didn't want to be stared at again by the attendants; but beyond this, although he had looked forward to seeing the Exhibition, and particularly his own modest part in it – the screens and photographic arrangements – with new eyes, he found, now that the moment had come, that he could not quite do it. Suppose he lost his head completely and stood there shouting out: 'All is not gold that glitters! Please form an orderly queue in the reverse direction! Your money will be returned at Admission and the Director of the Museum, Sir John Allison, will be found kneeling on the steps to apologise!'

This kind of thing wouldn't do, although it was no more than a nightmare. He would go to Ithaca Street.

The afternoon was so dark that the lights were already on in the little bookshops and translators' bureaux and undemanding cafés which had gathered under the august protection of the Museum. The Megaspeilon seemed barely to do business at all. It was a hole in the wall, and the unhopeful Greek proprietor indicated with a nod that you could walk straight through, move a pile of crates aside, and go up the dark staircase to Mr Coker's place.

'Place' was a very accurate description of Len's present home, for it had location and not much more. It had a floor, covered with what appeared to be sacking, but the walls were damp and the ceiling was suspect. Ingenious and neat-fingered, Len had fitted up systems of pegs on which his clothes and cooking-pots were suspended, and herbs, rather too optimistically, were hung up to dry. But the furniture was rudimentary, and Professor Untermensch was sitting by the gas-fire on a packing-case.

In the opposite corner was a large double bed, covered with a patchwork quilt; Len, in functional mood, had sawn off the legs, so that it was flat on the floor. I didn't know Len was living with anybody, Waring thought. I'll ask him about it, but not while the Professor's here. There was no sign of her, whoever she was, except for the patchwork quilt itself; Len could never have made that.

'Here we are, two unemployeds,' cried the Professor gaily. 'I am happy to see you again!'

'Hullo, Waring,' said Len.

'Len, before I say or do another thing I want to apologise to you. Ever since last Thursday, I've been under the impression that you tried to strangle me.'

'No, you've got that wrong, cock. I didn't strangle you, I put a fish-spear through your foot.'

'Someone did, though. Someone put a bit of string round my windpipe last Thursday night, at the Museum, down in the Exhibition.'

'You came back then, did you? I was in the hall when you went out.'

'I had to go down to the exhibition, and before I knew where I was I felt someone throttling me. I've only just discovered it was Hawthorne-Mannering.'

'I wouldn't have thought he had it in him,' said Len. 'Still, I'm a bit upset that you had this thought about me. A mishap with a fish-spear is quite another thing.'

'I know, I'm sorry.'

'Forget it. I was just about to make some Nescaff. Typical of unemployeds. How was Russia?'

'But hasn't the Professor said anything about it?'

'Wittgenstein tells us,' said the Professor quietly, 'that when we communicate a feeling to someone, something which we can never know happens at the other end.'

'Evidently he hasn't. Well, honestly, Len, Russia was disastrous. But it's one of a lot of things I don't want to think about just at the moment.'

'They've got the police in,' said Len. 'I can guess how you're feeling about Sir William.'

'I didn't get the chance to have another word with him before I left. I wish I had. And then I had an idea – not at the time, but I've got quite sure of it since – that he wanted to send me a message.'

'How?'

'He gave me a clay tablet to return to Case VIII. A bit odd, when you come to think of it. When I went to look for it this morning, it had gone.'

'What made you think there was a message on it?'

'When I thought about it afterwards, it struck me it was different from the others. It was the same kind of clay, that pinkish clay, and it looked old enough, but the inscriptions were quite new-looking, as though they'd just been done.'

'They *had* just been done,' said Len. 'As to the tablet, don't worry about it; I've got it.'

With a casual air he went to a battered refrigerator on the half-landing, opened it, moved a couple of bottles of milk and produced Sir William's tablet. It was the only place he had to keep things, he explained.

'How the hell did you get it out of Case VIII?' Waring asked. 'I put it back and locked up myself.'

'I was pottering round the next morning and I found some keys on the floor,' said Len. 'Someone must have dropped them. You, perhaps?'

'And then poor Jones saw them in your studio and gave them back to Sir William. Didn't you notice they'd gone?'

'What if they did? Keys are material possessions – they come, they go. They won't be necessary to the society of the future. Everything will be open to the people.'

'Len, will you tell me why you helped yourself to that tablet? You didn't know anything about it.'

'Of course I knew something about it. I made it.'

'Made it! Whatever for?'

'For Sir William. He knew I was quite competent at making things. He drew the signs, the picture writing, and I made a plaster-of-Paris mould and stamped them into the clay. I dried it with the infra-red to hurry things up.'

'Did he come down to the studio, then?'

'Dousha did. She explained what he wanted. When the clay was dried out, Jones took it up to him.'

'What do the signs mean?'

'I don't know. That's what I took it back for, to find out what it says. The old man must have wanted us to understand it, but –'

'Here is where I may be of some assistance,' broke in Professor Untermensch.

Waring looked doubtfully at the little square of clay. It reminded him vividly of the moment when the old man had pulled it out of his pocket with the handful of gold coins. That had been another deception, but this time one that was easy to forgive. It struck Waring that the tablet, hand-made to order by Len, had been in fact the only genuine thing in the Exhibition.

Professor Untermensch, usually so unassuming, held out his hand for the tablet, a master on his own ground. As soon as he began to explain the hieroglyphs a strong current of excitement, generated from the love of knowledge simply for the sake of knowing, made itself felt in the darkening room.

'We begin with the ideograph of the eye – in Garamantian, *wa*,' said the Professor.

'How can you possibly tell how they pronounced it?' Waring asked. 'Isn't it true that all we know about their language is that it sounded like bats squeaking?'

'The high twitter of birds, or the shrieking of bats,' corrected the Professor, 'but we have arrived at the sound values by a stroke of good fortune, not unlike, in a sense, that which enabled Champollion to translate the inscription on the Rosetta stone. I was lucky enough to discover, in one of the lesser-known mimes of Herodas, a passage in which a comical character, a eunuch, buys a Garamantian slave

(wa)   (Ro)   (phot)   (ik)

(poo)   (dump)   (lib)

(sog)   (hak)   (kut)

(phRu)   (wa)   (skwa)

and tries to give the equivalent, in Greek letters, of the strange sounds which he makes.'

'Wa!' said Len, bringing in Nescafé in three of the Museum's cups.

'Wa!' Untermensch repeated. 'This, of course, is the popular, not the sacred or hieratic language, which would be unsuitable for a personal message. We have next the metal pitcher, or brass can for water-carrying, *ro*, followed by an interesting symbol of two men side by side, carrying goods, which we call "the buyer and seller". The Garamantians had one word only for "to buy" and "to sell".'

'But surely they must have known the difference?' said Waring.

'It seems that they did not, and that this was one of the factors in their economic decline as a nation. I have written a thesis on the subject.'

'How does the word sound?'

'*Phot!*'

'*Wa ro phot . . .*'

'It is musical, is it not?'

'But not much like a bat,' said Waring.

'Ah, we do not know the intonations. Next comes the linking word, our "and", represented as a bridge, *ik*, and after that three identical little birds, *poo*, that is the repetition word, the equivalent of "re." *Poo-phot*, you see, would be *to buy again.*'

'Or to sell again,' said Len.

'Of course. Now, look closely at the next symbol. It represents the village-hall, or folk-hall of the Garamantian elders, where they held their weekly deliberations on affairs of state.'

'Did the King follow their decisions?' Waring asked.

'He ignored them completely. Yet here we have at least the machinery of democracy.'

'What's the word for this folk-hall?'

'*Dump.*'

'*Wa ro phot ik poo dump . . .*'

The Professor's face was transfigured, like one listening to distant music.

'Next we have a beak, *lib*; then *sog*, which may be either east or west, for we cannot tell whether the sun is rising or setting; then the sign *hak*, that is, stew.'

'What did they put in their stew?' Len asked.

'*N'en discutons pas*. Let us pass on to the next sign, which is of great socio-historical and medical interest: *kut*, the physician or surgeon, who is portrayed as removing the heart from a satisfied patient.'

'He's taking it out of his stomach,' protested Waring.

'Medical science must proceed by gradual experimentation,' replied the Professor, frowning at the implied criticism of Garamantian culture. 'Next – *phru*, all, or everyone, shown as a crowd of persons of different sizes; then – '

'*Wa!*'

'Ah! You learn quickly! What it is to be young! But after *wa* is the most poetic symbol *skwa* – the creative power of the Sun – the Sun-god Hobi gives life by breathing upon a plant.'

'He might be killing it,' said Len.

'That is so. Let us proceed.'

'With some of these you are familiar – *wa*, and the beak, *lib* – how much they thought about birds! The next sign is a loom, it is *dmin*, to weave – evidence of a higher craftsmanship! – '

'And *phru* meant "all" – '

'Yes – the Garamantians could not count beyond five. They used the fingers of one hand only. Hence "five" meant also "a vast number".'

Len sighed. 'You wouldn't get much accuracy that way.'

The Professor's spectacles flashed. 'A most curious sign next! An indication of an exceedingly high level of culture! The mummer, or mime – remark his strange chicken-like head-dress! In many of the caves in which such a sign has been found, the nose has been daubed red!'

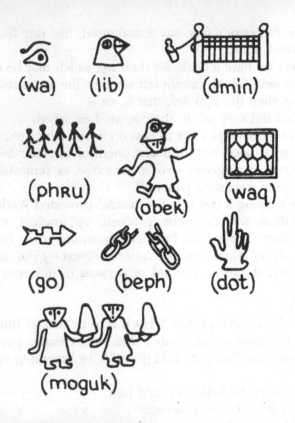

(wa)   (lib)   (dmin)

(phru)   (obek)   (waq)

(go)   (beph)   (dot)

(moguk)

'How's it pronounced?'

'*Obek.*'

'Two syllables at last!' muttered Len.

'Next, honey, a picture of a honeycomb, *waq*; *go*, simply a directional sign, meaning "towards" or just "to", and after that *beph*, "free", beautifully represented as a chain breaking in half; then *dot*, "to add", on the fingers of course, and that is what is shown here. The next picture is of the ambassadors, who come bearing tribute in the form of salt. I have shown that this sign is *moguk*, the embassy, or mission.'

'The ambassadors are drawn just the same as the Garamantians,' Waring pointed out. 'Wouldn't they look different, being strangers?'

'In the noble philosophy of Garamantia, as far as we can tell, all men were regarded as alike.'

'Classical Marxism,' said Len.

'Even the Golden Child?' asked Waring.

'You must not confuse the sacred and the mortal. The Child was sacred, and had to be buried apart. But to proceed with our message:

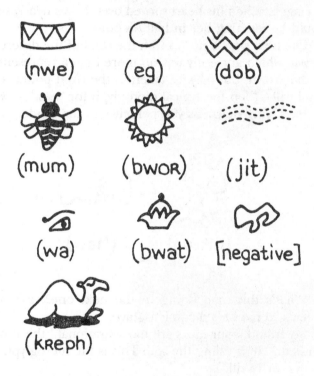

Nwe represents the teeth, or a tooth, it stands for either; then *eg*, an egg.'

'Rather a coincidence, that,' said Len.

'We shall find these congruences often in the study of languages. It does not do to attach too much importance to them. *Dob*, the sea – a wonderfully good representation of the sea by a people who had never beheld it but only knew of the Great Water by hearsay. *Mum*, the honey-bee; *bwor*, the past tense of "to shine", therefore, "shone".'

'What was the present tense?' asked Waring.

'There was no present tense. The Garamantians had no conception of the present. They thought only of the past and the future; hence, they were happy.'

'That wouldn't make me happy,' Waring said, thinking of Haggie. Then his heart turned over. It was nearly six. He would be meeting her in half an hour.

'The next sign is *jit*, "sand", the sand of the desert – *wa* – *bwat*, which anciently was no more than a representation of the crown, but may be taken as the royal power, or the royal will – then the typical hieroglyph for "rest" – *kreph* – a camel lying down, as you perceive, in the shade.'

(nit-og)   (haw)

'What's this man doing in the next one?' asked Len. 'Seems to me he's digging a grave.'

'My friend, your ideas are too sensational,' the Professor replied. 'He is tilling the soil. This is the hieroglyph *nit-og*, to dig, or to till.'

'And then we've got a handshake.'

'Certainly, the agreement sign, *haw*. At the end of a message such as this, it would mean "This is accomplished"; or "This is done." Below that is a seal, stamped in the clay, which was accepted for more than fifty years as Sir William's mark of authority, and was respected throughout Africa and the Middle East.'

'WA RO PHOT IK POO DUMP LIB SOG HAK KUT PHRU WA

SKWA WA LIB DMIN PHRU OBEK WAQ GO BEPH DOT MOGUK
NWE EG DOB MUM BWOR JIT WA BWAT [negative sign] KREPH
NIT-OG HAW. That's what I make it,' Waring said, 'and then
Sir William's special mark. How does it translate into
English, though?'

'That is what I have been asking myself. The ideographs
are absolutely clear; yet I confess myself baffled. Arranged
in this order they mean nothing, and absolutely nothing!
For so many years I have pictured to myself that if I could
step back in time, to the fifth century before the birth of
Christ, and if I were then to fall in with a Garamantian, let
us say in some forum or market-place, I could converse with
him instantly in his bat-like language. There would be no
barriers. Now I begin to lose confidence in my dream.'

'Perhaps we ought to read from right to left?'

'I have never known an instance. Still, I have tried, and
I have tried rearranging the symbols. I have even asked
myself whether Sir William had become confused with
ancient Egyptian, or with Chinese, where many of the signs
are determinatives. The sign for a pot, then, would not be
pronounced, but would simply indicate that the following
word meant some kind of liquid.'

'I doubt if it's as complicated as that,' said Waring. 'Sir
William must have done it pretty quickly, and I don't think
he knew Chinese.'

'Perhaps, just a suggestion,' said Len, 'he didn't want us
to bother about these actual signs at all, but only about their
transcriptions into English letters? WA RO PHOT and so on
– that could be a cipher of some kind, just as it stands. WA
recurs, for instance, and it might represent a single letter
– that would make it a very short message, though.'

'The English letters only?' wailed the Professor. 'What
then becomes of my ideographs? What is the fate of my
signifiers?'

He seemed deeply distressed, and both Len and Waring,
touched by the grief of pure scholarship, felt it their duty
to put the tablet aside and console him. Waring, however,

was anxious about the time; he had to meet Haggie at half-past six, that was agreed, and of crucial importance. He left Untermensch disconsolately huddled on the packing-case, with the inscrutable tablet still in his hand.

Waring walked fast, but he soon heard Len's footsteps thundering after him.

'Look, I hoped I'd catch you up, there's something else I wanted to ask you. I want you to come with me somewhere. Well, I want you to come and see Dousha.'

'Dousha! Whatever for? I've no idea where she is, anyway.'

'She's in hospital.'

'I'm sorry about that. What's wrong?'

'They took her into the Bedford Maternity. They think there might be something wrong about the baby. He's due in three months, May the 10th by my calculation.'

Waring stood still in the middle of Bedford Square. 'Len, do you mean it's yours, this baby of Dousha's?'

'Why not?'

'It's just the idea takes some getting used to. You care about Dousha?'

'You could put it that way.'

'All this time at the Museum you've been like that with Dousha? But she's not your sort. She's not socially alerted. She's soothing, undemanding, overweight, lovely, and brainless.'

'I know. That's why I like her.'

'Well,' said Waring. 'Congratulations.'

'I'm lucky. Not environmentally, not socio-economically, but from a sex angle, I'm lucky. I'm well aware that we're very different types, but egalitarianism doesn't mean that all partners must be similar. That's another bourgeois delusion.'

'So is jealousy, I'm told. Is that why you stood in the hall and stared like that when I took Dousha out last Thursday?'

Len hesitated.

'I admit that I wasn't so keen on your taking her out. Just an individual reaction. It passed.'

144

'Well, I'll certainly come to the hospital with you. Any other time. But I can't now, I'm meeting Haggie. And besides, on a visit like this, when Dousha's ill, you don't want me around the place.'

'I do,' replied Len, 'or I shouldn't have asked you. The truth is I haven't got the courage to go and hear the news by myself. I'm scared we've lost the baby.'

Waring had never seen Len look like this. He had looked genuinely sorry about the fish-spear, sorry about Sir William, but not like this.

'I could do with you with me,' Len repeated. And then he added, 'I felt a bit sick, you know – well, hurt, really – when you said you thought I'd tried to do you in.'

Waring recognised the force of the moral blackmail in this. Was he never to be allowed to choose his own life, and rather, when was the last time he did so?

'I'll come with you,' he said. 'You'll have to wait till I ring up home.'

He entered the battered telephone-box with a sense of recurrent fate. Haggie answered quite enthusiastically. She wasn't certain about her hair, and she was a bit behind time, having decided to make a new skirt at the last moment. When Waring put it to her that, this being so, they might meet, say, an hour later, she asked if he was going anywhere else, first, and when he said he had to, she asked if it was anything to do with Dousha.

Why had he never learned to tell lies, even lies of an ordinary everyday nature, to Haggie? Couldn't do it, didn't know how? Mention of the hospital made things worse. It was one of the worst conversations, altogether, that he had ever had.

'All right, Coker, you've ruined my life,' he said, as he came out of the box. He had put in 10p, but it hadn't been necessary. Len was sitting on a bench, waiting underneath the bare trees.

'Shall we go?'

'I suppose so. I'll have to get home afterwards as soon as

I can. That's crucial.' They began to walk together towards the bus stop. 'Are you human, Coker, or are you a wrecker? Why do you do anything you do? Why did you grow that cannabis? Don't tell me Dousha wants it!'

'Oh, that! I told you it was a disgrace – no, it was a crime – that the technical staff weren't allowed to investigate some of the samples that came with the Golden Child, the burial goods, the traces of wine sediment, the traces in the Milk Bowl, the seeds and so on. Opportunities were being passed by. In all fairness I had to get hold of a few seeds from the unpacking, and try them out.'

'How did you get them?'

'Oh, Jones managed it. Sir William thought they ought to be available for experiments too, and that was good enough for poor old Jones.'

'And then you planted them?'

'Yes, I borrowed a few pots from Funerary Art. I've got a mate doing Tropical Agriculture at University College; he lent me a hand. He germinated seeds in the labs over there. They came up as *cannabis indica*.'

'You told the police you grew it. Why didn't you tell them where it came from?'

'Not their business!'

Len pursued his own thoughts for a while, and then burst out. 'Anyway, it was the cannabis seeds that made me realise that the whole Exhibition was nothing but a hoax. Now, it's against my principles to let the People be deceived. But I don't like them to be disappointed either. I thought best to keep quiet.'

In spite of his misery, Waring felt a great relief in discovering that Len knew so much and, like himself, had decided to say so little.

'Did you do any more experiments? I mean, what about the sediment in the cup – the sacred royal wine, two thousand years old or more?'

'I had a go at that, yes. I rehydrated some of it.'

Their bus was rounding the corner.

'What did it turn out to be?'

'Pepsi-cola!'

They were in the hospital, going up an inclined passage with glimpses of clattering sluices and pantries. Turning into Pre-Natal, they were suddenly surrounded by beds full of women expectant of visitors, sitting up in floral night-dresses, looking at them hopefully, and then, as they passed, accusingly. They sighted Dousha at the end of the ward, smiling at them from a nest of pillows. The news was good, she was better, the baby would not be born prematurely, but was safe. Len gave a deep sigh, as though he had nothing else to live for.

'The doctor told me I was not to worry my head,' she added.

'I hope he hasn't been talking to you like a second-class citizen?' said Len, with a flash of his old spirit.

Dousha turned to Waring. 'When I heard about Sir William, I thought of you at once. It must have been very hard for you to come back and find him dead.'

Brainless Dousha had a gracious instinct of sympathy. Just for a moment Waring could not help wishing that Haggie had said something to him like that.

'He left us some money, you know, a little,' she went on. 'You, and me, and poor Jones. Most of the rest, of course, was for Sir John to buy things for the Museum, but we came in the little bits at the end of the will. I typed it myself, oh, several years ago.'

It struck Waring that he had never actually seen Dousha typing.

The probationers were coming round, rattling thermometers. He was not wanted here anyway. He left Len and Dousha together to talk things over.

On the way back to Clapham he tried not to think of anything at all. The idea of Sir William's bequest he put out of his thoughts for the moment, as one must do at a time when money and affection will not lie down together in the mind. Speculation about his new job – and it was promotion, after all – could wait until he knew whether he had anyone to discuss it with.

There was no light coming through the stained-glass panel above the front door of his house. Haggie, of course, was gone. There was no note this time, no communication at all, not even from the Whitstable and Protective Building Society.

WA RO PHOT IK POO DUMP. The tap dripped. Other people, in other houses, played their radios. He was alone.

6

The next morning Len, who was an early riser, and grandly careless as to other people's habits, rang up just before eight o'clock.

'Hullo,' said Waring. 'How's the family?'

'Fine. Dousha's fine, William is fine.'

'William? And if it's a girl?'

'Wilhelmina.'

Len did not ask about Haggie, and indeed he rarely showed interest in anything that was not uppermost in his own mind.

'How are you getting on with WA RO PHOT IK POO DUMP?' he asked.

'Not at all. I've thought quite a lot about it, but I just don't know where to begin.'

'I've changed my mind about PHRU representing a single vowel, an "l" for example. I can't get anything for the other groups. We must get at it another way.'

'It's all very well for you unemployeds to carry on like this. I've got to get to the Museum. I've got to see Miss Rank, of whom I'm terrified, about my alleged new job.'

Len considered. 'So you're off to spend another day of your life as a cog in the machine. Well, I'll see you around. I'll have another look at the cipher, yes. In fact, I'll probably see you later today at the Museum.'

Waring was surprised. 'You don't want to turn up there, Len. Let's face it, you've been fired. They might throw you out. You expectant fathers have got to look after yourselves.'

'There's still one or two things there that interest me. I'd just like to take a look at them. Yes, I'll be round at the Museum today.'

Miss Rank was waiting with the air of expectancy, and of hovering between two existences, which marks those who are just about to go on three weeks' leave. Her typewriter was covered up, her house-plants had been sent down to a friend, a secretary of the same grade as herself, who would keep them watered, and she was wearing a green crimplene trouser suit, with matching rims on her spectacles. Waring found her more intimidating than ever. Nevertheless there was just, but only just, perceptible in her manner, certainly not nervousness, but the consciousness of having been recently nervous, like the echo of the sound of something thrown into the water, long after the ripples have closed over it.

Miss Rank said that she would put him in the picture. She understood that Waring already knew that she would be away for three weeks, during which time he would act as PA to the Director, on scale AP4.

'What am I supposed to do?' Waring asked. 'What shall I do about the typing?'

'I should hardly go away on leave without making arrangements about that. All his correspondence is to go directly to the typing pool. They will come up and collect it twice a day.'

'And his appointments?'

'His book is made up for the next month, and it is very full. In spite of his distress at Sir William's death, he is carrying out his programme as planned, and I hope he won't find it necessary to change any of my arrangements.'

'I see. Well, do I go with him to meetings and so on?'

'I can't see that you will be wanted. Sir John will be attending a number of high-level discussions, some about the Exhibition – it may be going to Washington as well as New York, and he will have to spend a few days in the States – and some about the whole future of the Museum service itself. He may possibly take one of the Keepers with him, the Director of Establishment, possibly, to brief him. There will be no necessity at all for you to go.'

It was clear that there was going to be nothing whatever for Waring to do. He felt like asking whether he should bring in his knitting, but did not risk it. Miss Rank continued.

'Your main duty, obviously, is to present your report on your visit to the USSR. The Director will fly in from Zurich at 15.12. A car will be waiting and he will come straight back to the Museum. The special additional late-opening continues today, and he and Security are both staying here till 18.30 to get an idea of how that has gone so far, so he will see you at 16.30 in this office. I understand that your report is confidential. I advise that you type it in double spacing, so that you can write in Director's comments easily and then retype an amended copy to hand in to him.'

Waring was dismayed at this last remark. His report was not typed out at all, indeed it was only in the form of very rough notes, some of which had possible solutions for WA RO PHOT IK POO DUMP written on the back of them. Furthermore, he had left them at home, not realising they would be needed today. Still he had time before 4.30 to do something about them.

He looked round the orderly shelves of reference books, the locked cupboards and the discreet filing cabinets.

'I certainly shan't have any clearing up and rearranging to do,' he said.

He was thinking nostalgically of his old office and his layout boards, on which cups of tea could be precariously balanced. His remark was senseless. Of course the Director's outer office was kept tidy. But, much to his surprise, Miss Rank's voice grew exceedingly sharp.

'Whatever is that supposed to mean?'

'It isn't supposed to mean too much. Not anything, really,' said Waring conciliatingly. 'I was just thinking, you couldn't possibly mislay anything here, obviously; your system works so well. I shouldn't think there's ever been anything you couldn't lay your hand on at once. You've never had to ask "Where is it?" '

Miss Rank hesitated for a moment. She was, it was clear, a completely truthful person.

'It isn't impossible for me to lose something,' she finally remarked, 'but it is exceedingly rare.'

Waring felt vaguely encouraged. He took advantage of Miss Rank's momentary admission of human failing to hope that she would enjoy her three weeks' leave.

'Where are you going?' he asked.

A strangely girlish expression, her holiday expression, came over Miss Rank's skilfully made-up face.

'Oh, to Russia! February wasn't exactly the time that my friend and I would have chosen for a holiday – and it was only last Thursday that I was asked to go – but since it suited the Director I agreed, of course – and then it occurred to me, actually while I was getting your tickets, why not Russia? It was very late to book, but we managed it, and we are both thrilled – we are both so extremely fond of the ballet.'

'Are you going with Suntreaders?' Waring asked.

'Their Luxury Fortnight, yes.'

'Well, perhaps you wouldn't mind my offering a bit of advice. If you're keen on the ballet, see that you put yourselves down for seats pretty early. Otherwise you may find that you have to go to the Circus.'

'The Circus! But surely, that is for little children!'

'I used to think so,' said Waring.

When Miss Rank – who, though quite a young woman, still wore the same kind of high-heeled shoes as Haggie's mother – had tapped her way down the corridor and was heard no more, Waring felt deserted. The grand offices overlooking the leafless elegant square were, without her tedious but reassuring efficiency, as oppressive as a royal burial chamber. Waring roamed about. The Director's office was locked. Nearly everything was locked. It was only an obscure sense of what was due to a first day in a new job that kept him there at all.

He sat down on Miss Rank's chair. The report, of course. He had better write the whole thing out; but for that, he needed – as indeed he had all day – a reasonable supply of paper. The little drawers on the left-hand side of the secretary's desk resisted him firmly. The bottom right-hand one opened, and yes, it was a stationery drawer. There was a pile of assorted blank sheets, top-grade quality. Reluctant to start on the report, idly putting it off, he turned them over one by one, even the piece of brown paper at the bottom, the lining of the drawer. Then he stopped in astonishment. There was a gleam of gold.

It was not coins, not jewellery, but a book about the size of a postcard, and marked Bookbinders and Illuminators Gold Foil. 24 pages. 0.00008 cm. HM Government Property. It was the glitter of the fore-edge which had caught Waring's attention. What was it doing at the bottom of the dutiful piles of correctly headed Museum stationery in Miss Rank's right-hand bottom drawer?

Wherever it had come from, it was Museum property, and it did not belong here. Miss Rank might have yielded – in fact, it looked as though she had yielded – to the universal human weakness for that element which the Middle Ages knew could never rust or lose its brightness, because it was compounded of all the elements, equally mixed. Miss Rank had not been able to resist the glitter of gold. Waring turned over the pages of the book; the inconceivably thin gold leaf was backed each time by a square of sticky paper. Each page was numbered. The gold leaf, turning in the early morning light, which fell at different angles on its darkness and brightness, was fascinating. He gave way to an impulse and blew gently on one of the mirror-like surfaces. Immediately the gold leaf shrank away and crumpled, like a living thing.

But pages 12-13 were missing. Waring checked again and again. They were not there.

Least said, soonest mended. The best thing would be to

take it down to Conservation and Technical, where it belonged, the next time he went down to the basement.

Waring put it carefully in his pocket. In honour of his first day as Personal Assistant to the Director he had put on his blue suit, which was kept for interviews and special occasions only. He could feel the slight thickness of the book through the smooth material.

At that moment the telephone rang. Surprised at having to do anything so practical, Waring answered it.

'This is Inspector Mace of the Metropolitan Police. I expect you know that we've been conducting an enquiry here at the Museum into the circumstances of the death of the late Sir William Simpkin? We've more or less concluded our work here and we're closing down our incident room, but before we do that, we should very much like the opportunity of a word with you. Could you step along to Room 617, sir? It's just a question of assisting the police.'

It was true that the two policemen were, not at all reluctantly, in process of closing down their incident room. The enquiry was, for all practical purposes, at a standstill. The doctors could only confirm that in their opinion Sir William Simpkin had died between eight and eleven o'clock on Friday evening, and that the immediate cause of heart failure was, in all probability, the shock of the impact of the shelves. It was almost impossible that they could have been closed on him after his death. In that case he would have been lying on the ground already, and anyone who came into the library, whether they wished him well or ill, would have had nothing to do but report the death. No, somebody trapped him deliberately, and hoped it might be accepted as an accident. Of course, it mightn't kill him; but they must have thought it worth trying.

A delicate approach by the Inspector to his superiors had again produced a warning that though the examination of the staff might continue, not too much must be said or done about the circumstances of the Exhibition itself.

The witnesses, if they could be called that, continued to repeat, with increasing emphasis, that they knew nothing. Hawthorne-Mannering insisted, as before, that he had no recollection of either time or place. It was Sergeant Liddell's opinion that this last-mentioned witness resorted to stimulants; he was taking a drop or two, he thought, to keep his spirits up. Impossible to get much sense out of him. But then, it was difficult to make headway even with the straightforward question of Jones. Deputy Security, who had been co-operative in every possible way, did not ever recall having heard Jones's Christian name. The Establishment records had to be consulted to find out that he was called Jones Jones. His landlady in Willesden seemed to know nothing about him. He had no current passport, and the papers that had been found on his body consisted of newspaper cuttings about Sir William and the curse of the Golden Child, and three football coupons. A blank there. Then there was what the two policemen thought of as the disappearance factor: sick leave, dismissal, trips abroad – surely a very high proportion among the possible witnesses? The Inspector had told Sergeant Liddell to check on Len Coker's whereabouts and to try to have a few words with Dousha. Here Liddell had been rather more successful, and would have a respectable report to make when the Inspector came back.

Came back, because the Inspector had been on a day trip to Paris. It wasn't the Sergeant's business to feel a grievance, but he admitted to himself that he would very much have preferred this visit to another day in the company of the Museum's sugar-cupboard. Mace had, of course, been away on business. He had gone for further consultations on the actions and behaviour of Rochegrosse-Bergson.

He returned a disappointed man. Inspector Mace was quite free of that pettiness which leads those who have just been abroad to make those who have stayed at home feel that they have missed something. Mace, in fact, declared that he was glad to be back in the superannuated gloom of the incident room. Paris had been a swindle.

It was, surely, not to the Inspector's discredit that he had looked forward to a decent lunch with his connection in the Süreté, something with a little garlic, plenty of butter and so forth; but he had touched ground to find Paris and its environs in the grip of a strike which had closed all the restaurants and bars and every place of entertainment. The police were also nominally on strike, but his acquaintance had come to meet him as a matter of principle and honour, and had driven him slowly back to Paris through the directionless traffic to the Quai des Orfèvres. Here the Inspector had to listen to a story of frustration. There was no question but that Rochegrosse-Bergson, under another name, had organised the removal and sale of paintings and valuable objects from the museum at Poubelle-sur-Loire. There was no question but that Poubelle had had to close the doors of their pathetically reduced Museum when it was discovered, after their Curator's departure, that there was virtually nothing left to show. Whether Sir William had meant to imply, at Thursday's conference, that he knew about these activities and had half a mind to tell the whole truth about them, could not now be ascertained. The only well-established fact was that when Sir William had mentioned his change of name, Rochegrosse-Bergson had looked first angry, and then frightened.

But whatever the suave anti-structuralist had intended to do on his return to Paris, he had changed his mind when he got there. He had issued through his publishers, Editions Verjus, a statement for anyone who might be interested in his movements. Far from denying his guilt in the matter of the missing Rembrandt he now gloried in it, and had decided to produce a book of reminiscences, *Sous-Mémoires*, which would explain his methods of removing art treasures and the spiritual benefit which he had gained from his prison sentence, when he had come into contact with thieves, pimps and blackmailers. Today, although still established in his luxurious flat on the rue Baron de Charlus, he regarded himself as belonging to the Other Society. His persecution by the British police, who were attempting to lay at his door the assassination of an old man who had evidently died in the course of nature, was but a symptom of the panic reaction of society to the new race of philosopher-criminals who had come to dwell among them.

Inspector Mace's friend at the Sûreté thought it quite likely that Rochegrosse-Bergson, before his new transformation into a philosopher-criminal, which dated only from this week, might easily have attempted to hasten the death of the inconvenient Sir William. Possibly he might have had the help of an accomplice. The French police themselves would not be sorry to see him in the nick. But the evidence would be hard to find. One had to be a very clever man to produce such nonsense as anti-structural anthropology.

'Clever enough to get on to a good thing, what's more,' the Inspector told his Sergeant. 'That's another item on their file at the Sûreté. Hopeforth-Best is diversifying into cannabis – thousands of acres planted in Garamantia – all up one bank of the Fertile Valley – millions of packs of smokes ready in case the anti-narcotics laws change overnight – all they need is a first-class agent to deal with the Common Market – '

'Rochegrosse-Bergson?'

'Who else?' The Inspector threw a gaudily coloured packet on to the table. 'They gave me this in Paris. Provisional design for the packaging.'

The Sergeant smoothed it out with his square hand. On the front the brand name was printed in gold: HOPEFUL DREAMS. Beneath it was a picture of the Golden Child, blowing smoke rings, queerly smiling.

'Very poor taste, in my opinion, sir,' said the Sergeant.

Inspector Mace sighed. He had been obliged, after a scanty meal at the automat, to fly back to London. He had achieved nothing. Worse still, he had exhausted the 'credit' which always exists, whether acknowledged or not, between professional colleagues. It would be his turn next to do something for the Sûreté, and yet he was no further forward at all.

Deputy Security, both of the policemen had long ago decided, was the only person about the place to whom they could turn with some hope of a reasonable discussion. If he was Director, he told them, he'd cancel all these special exhibitions, and declare half the staff – not the Union members – redundant. There'd be no lack of uses, he pointed out, for the resultant savings. To begin with, the whole place needed rewiring and replumbing.

'You've no conception of how antiquated it is. Just a maze of pipes. Take an example. You've been investigating the electric and water supplies to the library area – necessary routine work of course, don't get me wrong – and the result is that, as from yesterday, there's no water at all in the Temporary Public Restaurant.'

'Sorry to hear we've caused any damage,' Mace had replied. 'You must itemise it, of course, and we'll see that it's made good.'

'No hard feelings. I've installed a static water tank in the courtyard, and I advised the Director to double the price of tea so as to cut down the amount of water consumed. But Sir John isn't too interested in these day-to-day problems. I don't know whether you've found that?'

Nothing, it seemed, but frustrations and mishaps. And there was really not much, either, to be expected from an interview with Waring Smith.

'I'll do what I can,' said Waring, 'but the whole thing defeats me. It makes me feel angry. In common humanity, who could leave him hanging there between two lots of steel shelves?'

'You're familiar with the library, sir?'

'I didn't use it much, because I've been too junior up till now to be issued with a key. But I can't see that it's possible to trap anyone between those shelves by mistake.'

'And the Director's library?'

'Oh, that's private. No one goes in there but Sir John and Miss Rank.'

'Who does the dusting in there?'

'I've no idea, but perhaps Miss Rank.'

'Who appears to be on leave. But we understand that you yourself have just been appointed as his personal assistant.'

'Well, yes.'

'Perhaps you could tell us, then, sir, something about the contents of this private library of Sir John's? For example, were confidential files or reports on the staff kept in there?'

'I've no idea if he had any,' said Waring, 'but I should have thought they'd have been in the Registry.'

'Or documents of a more general interest, possibly of a secret nature?'

'I think there *were* secret documents in connection with the Exhibition,' said Waring cautiously. 'I know there were some, for instance, in Sir William's room.'

'That may well have been so,' replied the Inspector with a touch of bitterness, 'but a number of Sir William's papers were sealed by order of the Director as soon as the death was reported, and I understand that they were returned to the Foreign Office. We weren't given the opportunity of seeing them.'

Waring thought it best not to comment on this. The details of the Garamantian economy, the Russian loan, the international jealousy over the exhibition and the generous sponsorship of the Hopeforth-Best Tobacco Company were all perfectly clear in his memory. But he ought not to have known them, and he couldn't tell whether the Inspector did or not.

'So you can't really enlighten me about the contents of the Director's library,' Mace went on. 'Did you know that the window had been broken?'

'Was it? Surely if Sir John broke it he'd report it, and have it mended at once?'

'It was broken from the outside. We found that a square

of glass had been removed, fairly roughly, in the middle of the pane. You know how that's done, of course?'

Waring had no idea.

The Inspector did not enlighten him, but continued. 'Of course this attempted break-in, if that's what it proves to be, may have a number of explanations. Would you, for instance, say that anyone in the building had a grudge against Sir John Allison?'

'A grudge? Well, how seriously do you mean? I suppose it isn't possible for anyone to rise to a position like that without causing some sort of resentment. Everyone knows that Sir John has a certain amount of difficulty with the older Keepers of Departments. I don't think it's disloyal to say that. It's common knowledge.'

'Which ones in particular, sir?'

'There was some difference of opinion as to how this very generous bequest from Sir William was to be spent. Sir John is a world authority on seventeenth-century French art, but naturally everyone wants accessions for their own department. For instance, I believe there are several thousand Persian carpets somewhere in the basement which no one has time to catalogue, but Woven Textiles says he can't hold up his head at international conferences unless he increases his holdings. And Unglazed Ceramics is just as bad.'

'Are either of these persons likely to break a window, or something of that sort, simply to annoy the Director?'

Waring hadn't laughed for what seemed a very long time, but he felt like laughing now.

'They're both rather too old for that sort of thing.'

He imagined the two tottering keepers assisting each other on to a pile of valuable carpets and trying, with shaking hands, to smash the window with a potsherd.

'Well, sir, perhaps we could return to the death of Sir William, on the evening of Friday last. There's a small detail which you might be able to help us with. The whole question of his heavy smoking, of his refusal to go into the library, the fire precautions and so on – well, that's all come up time and again during our investigation. Now, I don't know whether you're aware that Sir William's pipe was found in the pocket of his coat, broken into two pieces?'

'No, I didn't know that,' said Waring sadly. 'I don't know much about the whole thing, really. I suppose he might have dropped it and broken it earlier on.'

'Possibly, but it was only half full of tobacco, and it had been lighted. Now, if he was smoking when he dropped it, the pipe would have been hot, and he wouldn't have been likely to put it in his pocket. If it was cold, though, he wouldn't have left the half-smoked tobacco in it, that is, if he was the kind of smoker who cared about the flavour of his pipe. Now, we've been told that you knew Sir William well. Would you say that he was the sort of person who looked after his pipes carefully?'

'Yes, I would. He only had one at a time. I think it was sent him every year by someone who admired him. I mean, he *had* plenty of pipes but there was only one at a time he'd really care about, and he enjoyed cleaning it and worrying about it. "Dear is the helpless creature we defend," you know.'

'I'm not sure if I do or not, sir. Poetry, anyway?'

'He used to quote that. He liked poetry, games, puzzles – all arrangements of words, really.'

The Inspector sighed. 'Some do and some don't. Well, so much for the pipe. There's another difficulty, sir, which I hardly think you'd be able to help us with, and that's the matter of the keys. Sir William must have got into the library somehow, but his keys weren't found, either on the body or in his office. Someone must have taken them.'

'I suppose,' said Waring slowly, 'the same person that trapped him between the shelves.'

'That's what we suppose too, sir. But it would be a stupid and pointless thing to do. It's simply creating a mystery and attracting attention to it. Wouldn't you say so?'

Waring did not feel competent to say anything.

'Now, a rather different angle. We know, of course, that

you were out of the country when Sir William's death took place. In the Soviet Union, is that correct?'

'Yes, on Museum business.'

'You went on a package tour?'

'Yes, I suppose that was the cheapest way. I'm not a terribly important person, you know.'

'Nice to see that the Museum tries to save public money,' commented the Inspector. 'Now, sir, what I'd really like to hear from you is a personal estimate of one or two of your colleagues. Needless to say, you aren't under any obligation at all to answer if you don't wish to.'

'Of course,' said Waring. But he felt the obligation close in upon him in a way he hadn't done in the house near Haywards Heath.

'Now, Mr Marcus Hawthorne-Mannering. You didn't work for him directly, but for some reason which we can't pretend to have got quite straight, his department, the Department of Funerary Art,' the Inspector glanced at his notes in momentary disbelief, 'was in some way responsible for the Exhibition, and so we can assume you know him fairly well?'

'Fairly, yes.'

'Would you describe Mr Hawthorne-Mannering as a violent person?'

'I think he strikes most people as very sensitive, rather diffident, perhaps.'

'But would you think it possible that he could be violent on occasion? We have a note here of a remark he made when we interviewed him: "I hated Sir William." Does that surprise you?'

'I suppose most people have the capacity for hate.'

'Have you personally ever had any experience of Mr Hawthorne-Mannering in a violent frame of mind?'

Waring stared at the sugar cupboard. But he would have to give some sort of answer. 'Not face to face,' he said.

He was relieved to hear the sound of the Inspector clearing his throat, which heralded, like the appearance of a new theme in a symphony, a change of subject. But he was disturbed when this subject turned out to be Len Coker. Understood to be dismissed from the Museum, charged with being in possession of cannabis ... associated with extreme Left-wing organisations ...

'I know all that,' Waring broke in, 'but it doesn't give anything like a true view of Len. You couldn't recognise him from that. He makes things, that's his business in life, and he only pretends to destroy them as a recreation. As to the cannabis, there's an explanation for that.'

'Perhaps you could supply one, sir.'

'No, you'd better ask him.'

Inspector Mace registered the fact that W. Smith and L. Coker appeared to be friends, therefore not much co-operation could be expected from either one of them about the other. He tried another tack.

'Miss Dousha Vartarian, Sir William's former secretary, is also on leave. She is, according to our information, about six months pregnant, the father of the child being, once again, Mr Len Coker.'

Waring was startled. 'Who told you that?'

'Miss Vartarian.'

'But when?'

The Inspector looked across at his Sergeant, who said: 'I visited the hospital yesterday evening, shortly after Mr Coker left, and asked if Miss Vartarian was well enough to see me. She said she was, and I raised one or two points.'

'What nationality would she be, sir, would you say?' the Inspector asked. 'Of Russian origin?'

'Her parents were refugees, but I've no idea what nationality she is,' said Waring. 'Why didn't you ask her? She won't mind telling you. She won't mind telling you anything. She's completely open and straightforward. She's not over-burdened with ideas, she's very good-natured, and she's too lazy to roll over in bed.'

The Inspector made a note, Waring wondered what of, and glanced at his list.

'Did you know Jones at all well? I mean Jones Jones?'

'Was that his Christian name?'

'Apparently, sir. Very economical.'

'I certainly didn't know him well, nobody did but Sir William. You got the impression that, although I think he was really supposed to work in Stores, he could go anywhere he liked and at any time. He wasn't, for instance, supposed to enter the Staff Library, but if he wanted to, he did.'

The Inspector made another note. 'We don't seem to be able to get much further with this man, sir.'

'He was a kind of fixture. The Museum feels strange without him.'

'Yes, sir. Well, that just about covers everything. Perhaps, though, you wouldn't mind taking a look at this.'

The Sergeant handed over the plastic case which contained the only police exhibit, a single copy of the bright yellow leaflets headed GOLD IS FILTH.'

'Ever seen one of these before, sir?'

Waring felt relieved at such an easy question. 'Oh, yes, I saw those fluttering about the main courtyard on the first public day. Sir William had got hold of one of them, as a matter of fact.'

'Did it distress him at all, do you think?'

'Not a bit. He was worried by the queueing, but that was a different matter.'

The Inspector seemed reluctant to put away the leaflet, 'A certain political undertone here, would you agree? "Those who look upon the Exhibition are Doomed, and yet they are paying 50p for the privilege". A direct criticism of the Museum, and by implication of the Director?'

'I suppose so, but it seems rather childish.'

'And you can't throw any light on who might have ordered them to be printed?'

Waring shook his head. The Inspector sighed. Then, returning the leaflet to the Sergeant, he said briskly:

'We shall be closing up our incident room this afternoon,

Mr Smith, but I shall be available at Bow Street Station. Here is the number, and my personal extension. Or you can ring Divisional Headquarters at King's Cross. If anything occurs to you that you think I ought to know, if you remember any little detail, no matter how unimportant it seems, don't hesitate to phone us. Our enquiries will be reopened after the inquest, but in the meantime we'll always be available.'

Waring got up. 'They didn't give you much of a room, I'm afraid,' he said to Sergeant Liddell on his way out.

'We're used to it,' replied the Sergeant. 'In our work we get to some pretty funny places.'

In order to collect his notes and the somewhat sparse material for his report, Waring had to go back to the desolate maisonette in Clapham and trail in to Bloomsbury once again. He could, to be sure, have written the report at home, but that would have been to invite a deep depression which he was determined to avoid at all costs. Once back, he realised that he could not face the seclusion of the Director's, or rather of Miss Rank's, office. Why not try to write his report in the Staff Library? He was quite well aware that he had a certain horror of the place, and that if he was not careful he would find it difficult to go in there at all. That was not the right attitude of mind.

One of the warding staff, whom he only knew slightly, was on duty. He was quite prepared to admit Waring, having recognised his new status.

'You've only just missed Mr Coker,' the man added gloomily.

'Mr Coker? What's he doing here? I thought he'd left?'

'He was just having a poke around, Mr Smith. There seemed to be something he was looking for ... The Director's back from Switzerland, you know. Let's hope he doesn't catch Mr Coker.'

It seemed to Waring that unfamiliar views of the Museum to which he had devoted his career were appearing hour by hour. Keepers of Departments smashing windows, the Director 'catching' Len in the library – where had the age-old dignity of the Museum gone, its serene confidence as the repository of the wisdom of the human brain and the skill of human hands? Could its consoling peace and order ever be restored?

The attendant continued to hold forth, in tones of the deepest melancholy. Mr Coker, although declared redundant, had wanted to have a look at the shelving, and measure that breakage in the Director's window. That still wasn't mended, but Maintenance could get down to it, now that the police had gone. Waring reflected that the man's whole attitude and tone of voice was getting very reminiscent of Jones. Perhaps Jones was immortal, or perhaps in every Museum or even every organisation there had to be someone like Jones.

He sat down at a desk in one of the bays, forcing himself not to avoid looking at the shelves. The next thing was to lay out his notes, paper and Pentel, and to persuade himself he had done something. He felt strangely unwilling to start on the report itself; still the quiet hour, stolen from the working day, gave him an opportunity to review his personal position. The expedition to Moscow, the glimpse of the true Golden Child behind the walls of the Kremlin, had introduced him to enormous problems which he could hardly be expected to solve; but then he was making his report to Sir John, and in doing that he would transfer the responsibility to someone who would understand it and act on it. Sir John would know what to do.

Then there was a possibility that he might be an object of suspicion either to the KGB, or to MI5, or both. This reflexion didn't worry Waring in the least. If anyone was detailed to follow him, they would soon discover that he was not an agent of any kind, that he knew nothing and could find out nothing; he couldn't even find his own wife. This idea caused intense pain.

To hear a soothing voice! Even for a few minutes, that would help. On the impulse he left his desk and rang up the Bedford Hospital. He was in luck. Dousha had been allowed up and could take his call in the ward.

'How are you? How nice! Oh yes, I am lively. But I had visitor I didn't expect. You should have told me.'

'Told you what? What visitor?'

'Mrs Smith.'

'But I don't know any Mrs Smith!' Waring paused. 'You can't mean Haggie!'

'Yes, that is right, she came this afternoon. At first it seemed as though she might not be very friendly, but after a while it was OK. We talked about things, and we laughed so loudly that Ward Sister asked us kindly not to.'

'But where is she now? Didn't she leave an address?'

Dousha found this question confusing. Haggie had left no address. But that, in a sense, was no longer important. Now that Haggie knew that Dousha was quite harmless, quite guileless, what might not the future hold? A physical sensation like the thawing of ice, or the melting down of gold, warned him that the worst of his troubles were over.

Suppressing the joyous disturbance which made it harder to concentrate than ever, he sat down again to the report. How ought he to start? It was largely a matter, after all, of leaving things out. The Director wouldn't want to hear about the Suntreaders. On the other hand, if he confined himself to the last few events of the trip, would he be believed at all? He laid out his picture postcards; in Russia you could only buy them in sets, and he had chosen *Moscow in Winter*. That was the Arsenal. That was the house off Bolshaya Pirogovskaya where Tolstoy had lived. That was the block where Professor Semyonov didn't, unfortunately, live at all. That was another view of the Kremlin. That was Dzerzhinsky Street where the Lubyanka was supposed to be. And, God in heaven, there was a crudely coloured post-card of the Clown Splitov. Waring shuffled the whole lot away, and for the dozenth time read through the library notices.

> IF YOU DISCOVER A FIRE immediately give the alarm and, if unable to leave the library, await calmly the working of the automatic extinguishers. Do not take any personal risk, and on no account attempt to remove the books and furniture. ACT QUICKLY AND DO NOT USE THE LIFT.

How could the patient and self-sacrificing person to whom the instructions must be addressed think of removing the books or even using the lift if he couldn't get out of the door? Catching sight of another notice, which told him to work quickly in order to save electricity and fuel, Waring drew his unintelligible notes towards him and began desperately to write.

Just before half past four, with his report, still untyped and in a wretched condition, under his arm, he was in the corridor leading to the Director's office, passing the tall greenish pane of glass which was now known to all the staff as Jones's window. It had been sealed by the police, so that one could no longer open it and imagine how the dreadful drop, like a cliff's face, to the well of the inner courtyard must have looked to the unfortunate man as he leaned out and began his sickening fall, only a few days ago. In the courtyard far below there were glimpses of the patient queue being turned away, one by one, from the Cafeteria, which, because of the trouble about the water supply, was to be closed every day now just at the time when people hoped to get tea.

'I shall give up my job at the Museum,' Waring thought. 'I don't want to be a personal assistant to anyone. Such as I am, I want to be Waring Smith, true to the spirit that walks inside me. They're giving me this promotion because they're afraid of what I know, but I'd rather work and see the results. We'll go to the country, to a provincial museum if we can. We'll get an even smaller house, trade in the mortgage, grow runner beans in the garden and have a baby, a son, and we'll support the local team and go to football every Saturday.'

But would he be allowed to do this? Would the Museum allow it? And the Museum, slumbrous by day, sleepless by night, began to seem to him a place of dread. Apart from the two recent deaths, how many violent ways there were in the myriad rooms of getting rid of a human being! The dizzy stairs, the plaster-grinders in the cast room, the poisons of conservation, the vast incinerators underground! And the whole strange nature of Museum work, preserving the treasures of the dead for the curiosity of the living, filled him, as he passed Jones's window, with fear.

There were voices in the Director's room. If he was in conference, Waring had better not go in, but it was strange that Miss Rank's careful appointment list should have broken down so early, and very strange that the voices should be so loud. In fact it was only one voice, a deep one, a man's, which was resonant enough to drown the others.

Waring knew the voice perfectly well. In utter bewilderment he crossed the territory of Miss Rank, knocked once, and went in. The Director was in his accustomed place, with his back to the light, at his rosewood desk. Opposite him, on the visitors' chairs, sat Len Coker and Professor Untermensch.

How had they been allowed in? Len in particular, wearing his all-purpose sweater and battle-dress, as though in readiness for the People's Revolution, looked quite inappropriate and yet altogether square and determined, as though in no doubt as to his right to be there.

'What are you doing here, Len?'

'That is what I have been wondering,' said the Director. His pale, glassed-in gaze was bent, as though on the only civilised presence in the room, on Professor Untermensch. 'I have been trying to extend the usual courtesy of the Museum to the Professor as a visiting expert. His interest in our Exhibition, when I first welcomed him a week ago, seemed to be most gratifying. It is beginning to gratify me less.'

The Professor said nothing.

'Why are you here, Len?' repeated Waring, uncomprehending.

'On your account,' said Len.

'But why?'

'You're in danger.'

The nightmare that had haunted the Golden Treasure had come to rest at last in the sanctuary of the Director himself. Waring recognised instantly that what Len had said was true. He *was* in danger, and had been perhaps ever since he returned from Russia.

'You say my newly appointed personal assistant is in danger,' said Sir John with distaste. 'May I ask from what, or from whom?'

'From you, cock,' said Len.

Sir John's reaction was curious. He made no move to have Len turned out, or to go away himself, nor did he give Waring any sign of recognition. He simply remained in his unbending pose, his head turned slightly sideways, so that his spectacles appeared as blank panes of glass. Waring felt a sinking of the heart. Sir John Allison, the remote figure of authority and unrivalled scholarship, under whom, for the past two years, he had been proud to serve, sat there, and said nothing, and let himself be called 'cock', because, as was frighteningly clear, he could not do otherwise.

'Jones fell from the window,' said Len. 'He fell from the window, just outside this very room. We were afraid Waring might have to go the same way.'

'I'm going to hang on to life,' said Waring forcibly.

'Unless you're pushed,' said Len. 'It would have to be that. You're too young for a heart attack.'

Waring stared at him, and then at the Director, who was still doing nothing at all to control this uncouth visitor but sat behind his desk like a noble effigy of wax, faintly smiling.

Professor Untermensch seemed far away in thought. His looks strayed round the room, to the winter dusk outside, then to a small demonstration screen for showing transparencies which was installed between the bookcases.

'You're too young to be suffocated,' repeated Len, 'like Sir William was.'

'Sir William Simpkin died of a heart attack,' the Director said calmly.

'And how was it brought on? And where?'

'You are probably aware that I was attending a dinner party at the time at the Café Royal. I can therefore hardly be expected to offer an opinion. I only know that when I returned to the Museum after dinner there was no one in Sir William's office. I assume he had gone down to the library by then.'

'Not the Staff Library. Why should he? He went to your library, your private one. *You* thought of it, *you* suggested it, *you* gave him permission to smoke – you were the only person who could. "Go on, dear fellow, smoke if you like." That wouldn't have mattered in the big library. In your little place it did; the safety devices were sensitive to the first trace of tobacco smoke. That still wouldn't have mattered to you or me. We could have breathed deeply and got out before we'd inspired the crucial 7% of carbon dioxide. Sir William was very old. He'd suffer at once from headache and confusion, the CNS would be depressed, he would lose consciousness and collapse. When you came in from your grand dinner-party he was in a heap on the ground. All you had to do was to move him into the Staff Library; he was light as a leaf anyway. He couldn't be left where he was. You mustn't be connected with his death in any way. And there had to be a good reason for his heart attack, so that there'd be no question of suffocation, CO_2 and so on. The shelves did splendidly. Just prop him up to look as though they'd hit him. Nothing to do with you, was it? Not your fault, right off your hands.'

'Coker, you are over-excited. You are a troublesome

left-wing subversive, at present under notice of dismissal. Like most poorly-educated people, you are bitter and prone to wild accusations.'

'I'm a craftsman. I can make things. You can only show them. I've done my apprenticeship, I don't need your job. I can get another. But I don't like not knowing about things. That's how I found that the carbon dioxide had been discharged in your library.'

'The library has been sealed off by order of the police,' said Sir John.

'Not since they closed the incident room this afternoon.'

The Director, it was clear, had not realised this. He was taken aback, but he turned on Len again.

'But to my library, my own private retreat, you had no key!'

'I had Sir William's. You lent him one yourself on Friday night. You must have done. Had you forgotten that? You never took it back. That was careless. Jones brought all his keys to me after he'd been called in to see the body. I'd had them once before, as a matter of fact. Sir William didn't believe in secrecy, and he didn't believe in keeping people out of things. Jones knew that.'

'So you spied in my library. Well, it may be of interest to you to know that the police made a thorough examination, and no report was made of any trace of carbon dioxide, or any other contamination of the atmosphere.'

'Of course it wasn't. You let it out. You went round outside and made a hole in the window. Your window! I had a look at it. You used the oldest trick in the book, if you want to break glass without noise. Where did you pick it up? You a put a square of sticky paper, anything adhesive, in the middle of the pane, and give it a sharp tap. The glass breaks under the paper and you can lift it out quite easily.'

'And where do you suggest,' said the Director, 'in the middle of the night, I could find a square of adhesive paper?'

'Here,' said Waring suddenly. He took the book of gold leaf out of his pocket. 'You used the two middle pages.'

'Ach, my book of gold leaf!' cried the Professor. It was the first time he had spoken. '*Meine goldblätter!* I have been granted them by the Museum for my demonstration! I have demonstrated to you, Sir John, after the conference!'

'Where did you find that?' the Director asked, turning his glassy look towards Waring.

'In Miss Rank's desk. The right-hand bottom drawer.'

'I told her to throw it away!'

Waring could hardly recognise the intonation. All the habitual marble calm was gone.

'She didn't throw it away,' he said. 'She had a weakness, after all . . .'

'Few are those that can resist pure gold,' remarked the Professor.

'. . . and then she couldn't remember where she'd put it . . .'

'Miss Rank lost something! She disobeyed my orders!'

The treachery of Miss Rank had produced the first real crack in the superb edifice of self-value. The Director's hands went under the table, perhaps so that they should not be seen to tremble.

'And where is this glass and gold paper supposed to be now? The police made a thorough examination, I suppose, of the courtyard, and found nothing?'

'But Jones did,' interrupted Len. 'He looked before they did. He found the glass and paper, he understood what it was, and brought it up to show you. You took it from him and pushed him out of the window.'

'He tried to rise high,' said the Director in a yet stranger voice, 'and he fell from high.'

'What did it matter to you if he was smashed to pulp?' shouted Len, 'What did it matter to you if the whole staff of the Museum were under suspicion of a murder which you committed, simply because you were greedy for money?'

'If I suggested that Sir William should go down to my library, what could that conceivably have to do with money?'

'He was making a new will, and you knew it.'

'A new will? He may have made a dozen!'

'But this one revoked the bequest he had made to you on behalf of the Museum,' cried Professor Untermensch, 'and directed a totally new disposition of the moneys. He put to you the whole idea. He read it out, and then proposed a little joke to you.'

They were laughing and talking together that morning, Waring thought. Everyone in the Museum knows that.

'Childishness!' said the Director.

'Certainly. Childhood and old age draw near together. He liked to play games, or perhaps he liked to indulge those who thought he liked to play them. Would it not be a great joke to hide the new will somewhere, as in a romance? To hide it, perhaps, between some books? And you agreed, *ja*, it would be so funny. So prankish! You indulged the old fool! Why should he not hide the will in your personal library? That copy, we may be sure, you have destroyed when you have gone down to find Sir William's dead body.'

'And if so,' said the Director, 'what other copy can exist?'

After a moment, they heard a sound which only the Director recognised: the Professor's laugh. It was not loud, but it came upon them uncontrollably, breaking the silence.

'Ah wah hah hoo! Ah wah hah hee!'

The laugh died away, and Untermensch added, 'We have been able to decipher the tablet.'

'What tablet?'

'The tablet which Sir William Simpkin had made by this young man Coker, and which he directed this other young man, Waring Smith, to hide among the Exhibits.'

'That!' Sir John cried. 'That tablet is meaningless.'

'So you tried to decipher it!' said Len.

'I may have glanced at it. At the present moment it seems to be missing from Case VIII.'

'One of your exhibits! And you haven't demanded a

thorough inquiry? Why not? Because you're afraid to have it found?'

'I have told you, it means nothing! I believe it to be nonsense. How dared the old fool put it into my major Exhibition?'

'Why shouldn't he? He knew your major Exhibition was nothing but a mass of replicas and fakes!'

'He knew that!'

'All the time. That's why he wouldn't bother to go down and see it.'

'He fooled me! He never told me! The lying old bastard, the snivelling old Judas!'

This was altogether too much for Waring.

'Don't speak about Sir William like that!'

Waring sprang up, and stood, with his job and his career and all his convictions at stake, in front of the great Director. There is no language like the language of the heart.

'He's dead. You did it. I don't know why you did it. But don't talk about Sir William like that. Shut your mouth, or I'll shut it for you.'

'*Schauen, bitte!*'

The shrill command from Professor Untermensch turned all heads towards him. In the room, now almost dark, the little demonstration screen sprang into light. Greatly magnified, the image of the tablet with its ideographs appeared before them.

'You are correct, Sir John, the inscription cannot be deciphered,' said the Professor, taking up his stand, and falling into the commanding tone of a lecturer, 'not, that is to say, from the Garamantian language itself. The solution, however, has been proposed to me by Mr Coker, after he had worked for several hours on the decipherment. We are not to look at the sounds which the ideographs convey, or the English alphabet in which we write them, but rather at the concepts which are pictured in the characters themselves; follow me closely.' He glanced commandingly round his strange audience of three. 'EYE / CAN / SELL / AND /

RE / FOLK-HALL / BEQUEST / STEW / SURGEON / ALL / EYE / SUN / EYE / BEAK / WEAVE / ALL / MIME / HONEY / TOWARDS / FREE / ADD / MISSION / TOOTH / EGG / SEA / BEE / SHONE / SAND / EYE / WILL / NOT / REST / TILL / THIS IS DONE /'.

In the Professor's mingling of accents the reading of the inscription sounded strange indeed.

'I cancel and revoke all bequests to Sir John Allison. I bequeath all my money towards free admission to the exhibitions and I will not rest till this is done.'

'Mumbo-jumbo!' cried the Director. 'Meaningless gibberish, unwitnessed, without the slightest importance in law!'

'Except as evidence of his intentions,' replied the Professor, stepping into the brilliant light of the projector, 'but Sir William, I think, would not be so foolish as to rely on such means. They were, as we have said, a little joke for you both to share. You will doubtless find that he had deposited a perfectly correct and legal version of his will, let us say, in one of the banks of Zurich.'

'You have no reason to think that!'

'But you have, haven't you?' said Waring. 'That's why you flew to Switzerland yesterday?'

'Not much gibberish in Swiss banks,' said Len. 'Bastions of capitalism, but they know how to look after a will.'

The Director took his eyes with difficulty away from the screen. He had been staring at the ideographs with a kind of cold nausea. Now he appeared to pull himself together for a supreme effort.

'And even if this is true – even if Sir William had withdrawn his confidence and no longer desired me to have control of the sums which I could have spent so wisely, so profitably – even so, what evidence, what possible evidence, could be brought to show that I planned his death? None! No material evidence whatsoever!'

'There'll be a hundred things you've forgotten, cock,' said Len. 'Jones may have said something to one of his mates before he came to see you. The carbon dioxide discharge is empty. Police mayn't have tested for fingerprints yet, but they will do after the inquest. You'll see. It will all close round you.'

'There will be fingerprints on my gold leaf,' said the Professor.

'And on his pipe,' said Waring suddenly, 'he'd been smoking, hadn't he – you said he could – but the pipe broke when he fell. You didn't know what to do with it, so you crammed it into his pocket, the two bits of it, to get it out of the way. That was another mistake. The police noticed it. But I wonder how you felt when you were doing it. He trusted you.'

'So much the worse for him.'

'He liked you. He told you about this will because he thought you had a mind above money, and could understand him and wouldn't mind a joke about it, as long as the Museum still benefited. You left him to suffocate there and you stuffed the pipe back in his pocket and dragged him next door.'

'None of this touches me. A great Museum is like a sovereign state at war. Only one can decide. And Sir William was not a Museum man. To him the holdings were a show to the public – a bazaar – a peepshow – a mere booth! He had no conception of the Museum as a great empire of objects to be preserved for endless time in ideal conditions, unseen, unpolluted, for which his money was needed – all his money! I have been spoiling him, and letting him live, for years. But I should never have allowed him to establish himself here. He was not trained in conservation – he was, after all, no more than an archaeologist – a digger! If he hadn't put spade to ground sixty years ago and turned up these half-savage golden objects, if he hadn't done that, then we should have been spared the present hideous nightmare, the public invading my museum to see what is no more than a roomful of fraudulent trash. Of that I accuse Sir William. I accuse!'

Deeper and deeper wells of hatred opened up before them as he spoke.

'But I have regrets. Not because I have eliminated a mischievous old man, not because I have killed a human being – neither his life nor mine could be put for a moment in balance against a single silver-gilt écuelle by Charles Petit! No, that is not the reason. No – I reproach myself because I have broken the rules of my profession and attempted something for which I was never trained. About French porcelain and silver I know all that a man can know. But I did not know how to commit a murder. I still do not know! I am out of my field!'

The Director was standing up. He was no longer trembling. He had a gun in his hand, a little Belgian automatic, glittering, but not like gold, a beautiful object, like everything else he possessed. Waring had never seen a gun close to before, only on TV, or under glass in the Museum. He was amazed that the Director had one. He had never seen a dead man either, or a man killed. There was a gentle thud of overturned furniture. Len, trained in Conflict Promotion, and the Professor, reared in Eastern Europe, were flat on the floor. The Director, holding the little gun, advanced. It was grossly out of place. The room was quite still, with an occasional sigh, perhaps from Untermensch, but it was as if the room itself were breathing deeply. Waring, like a diver, felt his senses immersed in what the Director was going to do. When the shot came, it was not as loud as he had expected, but he went down as if he had been struck by an express train. He was not dead – shooting was not in the Director's field either – but he was hit. He sprawled, and it must be his left shoulder somewhere, because, though there was no pain, he couldn't feel it at all. He got on to his hands and knees. It was his job to bring the Director down, and that was the only thing in football he had ever been good at, hooking some-one round the ankle. And that was a foul. He tried to crawl forward. But Sir John, elegant and efficient in all his movements, swerved past and out, and Waring, clutching his shoulder, saw him disappear, still with the gun, towards his private lift.

Rapid as the Director was, the Professor was before him, rising with a bound from the floor and sprinting, faster than he had ever done round the Circus Splitov, to intercept him as he reached the corridor. Waring, getting up heavily, conscious of blood running, first warm, then cold, down the inside of his shirt, saw the two of them as they came to Jones's window, Untermensch throwing up his arms as though in fright, then scurrying on, the pursued now, not the pursuer. Waring had no idea that he could be so agile, or that the Director could run at all. As he followed them, half-dazed, he could see only Sir John's back. A moment later he glimpsed the tiny Professor, swerving sharp right at the central staircase, then spinning round the first curve like a bundle of old dark clothes. No doubt about it now; he was terrified. Sir John hesitated, for a moment only, at the doors of his private lift, and followed down the stairs.

He won't shoot again here, Waring thought; they'd hear the shot all over the building. And indeed the Director's gun was back in his pocket. But, even without a weapon, he was a hunter. Better not to see the expression on his face.

Waring gripped the banisters, while the steps rose like a flight of marble bats to meet him. The clattering feet went on ahead. He felt sick to death. They were down a floor now. The familiar notice, the pointing hand: XXXIII – LI UNGLAZED CERAMICS. Never much visited, the long galleries stretched ahead, the floors polished to a high gleam. Nasty falls they'd get here, if they did come, Jones used to say. And now to Waring's horror he heard a series of smashes and crashes, some faint, some thunderous, as Sir John, still in pursuit, swept the exhibits from the open stands, felling the earthenware pots and stamping them under his feet. A great man, he was going mad greatly. His faultless white shirt-cuffs gleamed as, with deliberate sweeps, he dashed another £10,000 worth to earth. Years of patient work, of skilled restoration, lay in fragments. The Director ground them into dust. As Waring came to the entrance, he felt the littered floor crunching beneath his shoes like the Have-a-Go stall at a fairground. Then a giant pot, already unbalanced on its stand, slid and knocked him sideways, dowsing him with the rubbish that had been tipped into it, cigarette ends, paper, leaflets. Bright yellow leaflets showered out in their hundreds, and even in his moment of agony Waring's mind recorded: now I know where those came from.

Sir John stampeded onwards through the helpless ranks of pots. At the end of the gallery little Untermensch could be seen, stopping again to plead, but not for himself this time – begging the Director to spare the life of the beautiful objects. A fatal move, wasting vital seconds, and Waring, on all fours amidst the rubbish, tried to shout in warning. Cutting across his voice, a warning bell shrilled through every corner of the Museum. Forty-five minutes to go until Special Late Evening Admission Time.

Keeping his balance like a skater, Waring staggered the length of the floor to the next gallery. There was no one there. The two of them had vanished. He turned back. Try the corridor, he thought. And sure enough, someone was standing at the window, directly under Jones's window it would be, but this one was wide open, and as Sir John leaned out a great blast of wet and frosty air rushed in. Half over the sill, the eminent maniac was holding Untermensch by his two thin wrists, hanging him down outside while he sawed the wrists to and fro on the frame. The Professor's voice came only faintly:

'Spare me! I alone can read Garamantian!'

Was he heard? Surely it was the right plea, but the Director's face, seen in profile, was implacable, as though rejecting a piece not up to Museum standards. Quite gently he let go; gently he adjusted the white cuffs. A horrible high thin call came from the dark middle air.

Sir John, as though satisfied, made off once again for his

private lift, but Waring, knowing it was too late, sagged over the window-sill and stared down. There was nothing below that he could make out except a faint gleam, perhaps something whiteish. Whatever had fallen from that height was past recall.

The doors of the Director's lift clashed. What use am I, Waring muttered. The heavy old public lift, unreliable at best, wouldn't be unlocked for another half-hour or so. The stairs again, then.

'Bloody hang on. I'm coming. Where is he?' It was Len. Waring had almost forgotten him. 'Went wrong, thought you'd gone through Oriental. Where's the Prof.?'

'Not here,' answered Waring senselessly.

'Where, then?'

'The Director killed him.'

Len stood stock still. He saw the open window, and understood perfectly. Then he brought his two large fists together with a gesture as though wringing the neck of something hateful.

'You let him get away. Where's he gone?'

'To the Exhibition.'

'With his gun?'

'He didn't drop it.'

'You're sure he's in the Exhibition?'

'Where else? He has to go there.'

Waring's head was swimming. With Len to give him a hand he made better progress. They were at the foot of the stairs, through the falsely golden entrance hall, the blown-up photographs, the tablets, the sacred vessels, the jewellery; they had to wait, because of the barrier, to go one by one through the darkened triangular aperture to the central tomb. Waring felt blood running through his fingers, not too much, though; keep going. As they threaded their way through the locked and lidded cases they saw the Director flitting ahead of them; he turned, a spot-light picked him out, and he was seen to be without his glasses, with lidless pale eyes open like those of a nocturnal bird of prey.

'All fakes! In my museum! Replicas! Filth!'

And raising his little gun, he cried out, 'Be frightened!'

Waring lunged forward, staggered against him and caught him off balance. The Director seemed to spring sideways, to fly through the air, as he turned the gun on himself, fired one shot, fell onto the Golden Tomb with a force that shattered the central glass, the coffin of salt, and the inner shell of reeds and basalt, and revealed in place of the royal child a withered and starved little African who had died not long ago, but was no more than skin and bones, for it had certainly died of hunger.

'You're hurt,' said Len. 'Frankly, you're falling apart.'

'I'm in a bit of a mess,' Waring admitted, looking down at his shoes, which seemed to be full of blood. 'But I'll have to do for now. I wish I hadn't put on my suit, though.'

'It is wonderful, however, what dry cleaning can do,' said the voice of Professor Untermensch. 'One suit has already lasted me through several wars.'

The Professor, in fact, had come into the burial chamber and was standing just inside the door, soaking wet and crumpled – but when was he not crumpled?

'Why aren't you dead?' shouted Len, in tones of the deepest affection.

Waring felt his resistance giving way. Tears pricked somewhere at the back of his eyes in response to the miracle. 'Why aren't you dead?' he repeated stupidly.

'I was more fortunate than poor Jones. I fell into water. There was for some reason a static tank in the courtyard. Luckily the ice on it was melted by rain.' The Professor's eyes lighted on the crumpled body of the Director. 'But we are in the presence of death! Sir John is no more!'

'He tried to kill you!' Len broke in, but the Professor was unperturbed, and they all fell silent for a moment, as though their silence was a memorial.

'Look, Len,' said Waring with an effort – he was just beginning to feel an intense pain in his shoulder – 'I'll get a doctor and the police myself, they gave me a number, I'll ring through from the Duty Office. I want to know what we're going to do about the people, about the public. They'll be here in half an hour. It's the special evening opening.'

'We'll have to shut up shop, of course,' said Len. 'You Museum men!'

'I don't want that. We can't. They've been queueing for six hours, and it's raining and beginning to snow. You say I'm a Museum man, so was he' – they both looked at the twisted body of the Director, deep in shattered fragments of glass and gilding. 'I'm not having them kept out just because one Museum man went berserk!'

'Where could we put him?'

Len and Waring looked round to see the Professor measuring himself against a large and darkly-painted coffin, which, although thought to be of considerable value, had been propped against the wall to give an appropriate atmosphere. Waring knew it was labelled *Coffin of Uncertain Date, probably that of a royal Tax-Gatherer.*

'We might damage it,' he said.

'It is a replica,' replied Untermensch.

Len was very strong, and the Professor was much stronger than he looked. Between the two of them they lifted the Director, whose arms fell to his sides as they dragged him away from the case like those of a marionette or sawdust doll, and propelled him inch by inch into the shadowy recess where the coffin stood. Waring awkwardly took a handkerchief out of his jacket pocket with his good right hand, spread it out, picked up the fallen gun and wrapped it up. The lid of the coffin shut with a crunch.

'May he rest in peace!' exclaimed the Professor. 'The life of scholarship is dangerous!'

The late duty staff could be heard coming, with deliberate tread, through the approach room to open up. 'There's been an accident,' said Waring, going out to meet them.

'My God, Mr Smith, you've hurt yourself!'

'Well, in a kind of way, but the real accident was to Sir

John Allison. He's collapsed, I'm afraid. Yes, he's collapsed altogether.'

'Was it his heart, sir?'

'His heart has been affected by the accident, yes.'

'Do you want us to get on to a doctor?'

'You can leave that to me and Dr Untermensch, who was present when the accident occurred.' The word 'Dr' was effective; the attendants were reassured by the suggestion that Untermensch was medically qualified; and indeed, Waring reflected, quite possibly he was.

'Sir John would not wish the exhibition to be closed. He himself is resting peacefully. Let the public in as usual, but just hold them for a while, will you, while we sort things out?'

'How are we supposed to do that, Mr Smith? They're not in a very co-operative frame of mind. They've been standing in the rain for hours on end.'

Waring did not think, so much as let thoughts come to him.

'They have to pass the Ruskin Lecture Theatre as they come in, don't they?'

'Yes, on the left as they come up to the admission desk, but it's locked up, of course, we're not using it for the duration of the Exhibition.'

'Get it unlocked.'

Waring, for the first time in his life, found he had no difficulty in giving orders, and his orders, in turn, were being accepted without question.

'Get it unlocked, and divert the queue in there as they come. It holds three hundred, the rest must wait a bit longer. Tell them that before going into the Exhibition itself they're going to hear a very special lecture arranged . . .'

'Arranged for what, Mr Smith?'

'Arranged in honour of Sir William Simpkin.'

'A lecture? Who shall we say is giving it?'

Waring hesitated for only a moment.

'Mr Hawthorne-Mannering.' Pray heaven he's here, he thought. If he is he'll have to do it. He couldn't deny that he owes me something.

'Are they to be asked to pay for admission?' the Attendant asked. 'They're more likely to listen if they do.'

'Don't people usually listen to lectures?'

'Well, I don't know about Mr Hawthorne-Mannering's, sir. He hasn't done very much lecturing. He gave a series on Little Known Water-Colours of the Suffolk School last year. It wasn't too well attended.'

Waring considered. 'No, don't make them pay. It's all free. A wonderful opportunity. The only time it will ever be given. It'll hold them back for half an hour.'

Without allowing time for further discussion he went to the emergency telephone and rang through to Hawthorne-Mannering's private extension. A silvery voice answered. One had returned. Was the Director back from Switzerland? One had come back from sick leave especially to see him . . .

Waring took two minutes to explain what he wanted, and to silence, by the simplest form of moral pressure, the wail of protest at the other end of the telephone. Must he, Hawthorne-Mannering implored, really lecture on the Garamantians themselves? One knew so little – one simply hadn't enough material . . . One must in any case consult Sir John . . .

'You'll find that difficult,' said Waring.

'Is he down at the Exhibition?'

'Yes.'

'And he requires me to do this?'

'The situation requires it. And you owe it to me. And what's more, you know what I'm going to talk about, if you don't do it.'

He'll come, Waring thought, as he rang off. The late duty men were opening up the auditorium of the lecture theatre. It was as cold as the ninth circle of the Inferno. There was no hope at this time in the evening, he was told, when most of the maintenance staff were off duty, of getting the place heated up.

'You might play some music while they're waiting,' suggested Waring, 'the TA system in the auditorium will work all right.'

'I don't think there's any tapes down here, Mr Smith, except that Garamantian drums and singing. You remember you came down here on behalf of the Exhibition Department and told us not to play it for fear of affecting people's nerves.'

'Well, if that's all we've got.'

'Might give the public the creeps, sir. Might frighten the kiddies . . . '

'Play it! Play it until the lecture starts. It will be a new experience for them. And call an ambulance round to the back entrance.'

Len came out of the Burial Chamber room. 'The Professor's sweeping up the glass,' he said, 'that man's a miracle. He says he's used to it, the Nazis used to make him do the street-sweeping in Vienna in 1937.'

It was so. Untermensch, as though by instinct, had found the broom cupboard, and was clearing the litter with expert sweeps into a dark corner. The sound of the bristles on the wooden floorboards was soothing.

'Look, Len,' said Waring, 'how long would it take to repair the Golden Child?'

Len glanced rapidly, but professionally, at the broken coffin.

'First of all, it goes without saying, we've got to get this poor little skeleton out and give it a decent burial. Woking Mosque, if possible. Then the outer shell, the part that people see, we'd have to give it an armature, say wire and plaster, polystyrene won't do. Then we'd have to get down to making good the outer shell, exact scale drawings of the decorations from what's left and from illustrations, photographs and so on – then you could begin transferring the patterns – matching the colours is going to be almost impossible, then it's all got to be sized down, and the gold goes on last, of course, but the gold-work is all slightly raised above the surface – call it eighteen months, if we're lucky, or two years.'

'Two years,' said Waring. He pulled the book of gold-leaf out of his pocket. 'How long would it take you to patch it up to look good enough just for this evening, just for the two hours' public admission?'

Len took the gold-leaf and turned it over from one hand to another, pondering deeply.

'Can you find any newspaper?'

'I should think so. You didn't answer my question. How long will it take?'

'How long can you give me?'

'Thirty-five minutes.'

Waring went to see how things were going outside. It seemed that his instructions were being followed. An ambulance had been called, the crush barriers had been put out, and the first three hundred had been diverted into the Lecture Theatre.

'What about the rest of the queue?' Waring enquired anxiously, 'How are they?'

'Restive, sir.'

'Do you think they'll refuse to wait any longer?'

'Oh, no, sir, they're anxious for their turn. For the lecture, I mean. They can hear the laughter, you see.'

'Laughter? What laughter? Isn't Mr Hawthorne-Mannering in there?'

'Yes, he is, sir.'

'Well, what's he doing?'

'He's posturing, sir.'

Seized with a sudden dread, Waring threw open the door of the Theatre. There was no laughter at the moment, or anything like it. The whole auditorium, from top to bottom, was full of rapt faces. On the stage Hawthorne-Mannering, nearly naked, painted and gilded like a Garamantian of old, face hideously whitened, was executing a ritual dance step to the rattle and tuck of a small drum which he beat alternately with the palm and the side of his hand. From his lips came a rapid stream of sound almost too high for human ears, rising and falling like the demented twittering of a bat.

Without disturbing the mesmerised attention of the audience, Waring retreated after a few minutes and returned to the Chamber of the Golden Child. The Professor, after making a good job of the sweeping, had dropped off to sleep on the attendant's chair near the door. No doubt he was tired, and madness, death, and destruction were not a new story to him. Len had begun work. He nodded at Waring, giving instructions without turning away from the centre case. Waring was to wring out the strips of newspaper which were soaking in a bucket of water and squeeze them as hard as possible to make a kind of papier mâché. He handed the messy, grey, unpromising handfuls of wet material to Len, whose square-ended fingers seemed to act like a separate organism, moulding it into the cracks and corners to restore the broken shape of the inner coffin.

'I can't do anything about the outer one, the salt crystal one. That's all swept into a heap.'

Waring took the printed label from the case, turned it over, wrote OUTER COFFIN TEMPORARILY ON LOAN TO THE VICTORIA AND ALBERT MUSEUM, and then went back to his papier mâché. His shoulder was by now painfully stiff. He worked as much as possible with his right hand.

'There's a bit of red on the paper. Will that matter?'

'Yes, it's the *Exchange and Mart*. It won't show, not if I can get the gold leaf to stick. But the surface is too wet, it's going to be a poor job.'

'Just for two hours,' said Waring. A slave of the bucket, he squeezed, dripped and wrung, giving himself up to Len's unhurried proceedings. Len began to apply the gold leaf, brushing off, from long habit, the surplus gold into the bucket of water, so that it could be recovered later. The Professor slept on, the dead Director, propped upright, was shut in his sinister case, the Golden Child, in all its fantasy, was slowly reborn, piece by piece. Its gilded eyes seemed to wink, as though looking round for its missing doll.

Thirty minutes later the sound of the audience rising from their seats and leaving the theatre was checked by the voices of the warding staff; everyone must go back to the queue. From the cupboard which he had to share with the slumbering Professor, with Len, the broom, the bucket and the remnants of wet newspaper, Waring waited in trepidation for the first visitor. The tranquillising effect of the hard work had worn off, and he was now in great pain, and exceedingly frightened. He had lowered the lights until the Exhibits could hardly be seen, but even so, there was something terribly wrong, which must strike even the most innocent observer, about the Golden Child. The whole Museum seemed to be drawing in its breath to wait, with its two-hundred-year-old name and fame in the balance.

A patient-looking middle-aged family man, who must have been queueing now for more than half a working day, was the first, with his two exhausted little girls, to enter the Chamber. They hastened their steps as they turned the corner, glad to escape from the far from sane atmosphere of the Lecture Theatre. In spite of the directing notices, which in any case were practically invisible in the dim light, they went straight to the central case to see the long-awaited Child.

'Look, real gold!' said the man, turning to the open-mouthed girls.

'It looks almost new,' he added. 'It might have been done yesterday.'